"Loo

Bonnie began, only to have him interrupt.

"I think we've progressed to Frank by now, don't you?" His eyes slid meaningfully to the shelf where she'd put the sketchbook.

Her face turning scarlet, Bonnie decided to avoid names altogether. "I know what you must be thinking—"

"I doubt it."

He was as determined to fluster her as she was not to let him. Doggedly, Bonnie went on with what she had to say. "I know that I had no right to draw you without—"

"Clothes on?" he interjected. "Oh, I don't know..."

"Without your permission." She sent him a fruitless, silencing look. "But you see, what really happened is that only—"

Frank kept right on talking. "I just wish you'd have let me have the pleasure of doing the actual posing."

Dear Reader,

During this holiday season, as friends and loved ones gather for Thanksgiving, Silhouette Romance is celebrating all the joys of family and, of course, romance!

Each month in 1992, as part of our WRITTEN IN THE STARS series, we're proud to present a Silhouette Romance that focuses on the hero and his astrological sign. This month we're featuring sexy Scorpio Luke Manning. You may remember Luke as the jilted fiancé from Kasey Michaels's *Lion on the Prowl*. In *Prenuptial Agreement*, Luke finds true love...right in his own backyard.

We have an extra reason to celebrate this month—Stella Bagwell's HEARTLAND HOLIDAYS trilogy. In *Their First Thanksgiving*, Sam Gallagher meets his match when Olivia Westcott returns to the family's Arkansas farm. She'd turned down Sam's proposal once, but he wasn't about to let her go this time.

To round out the month we have warm, wonderful love stories from Anne Peters, Kate Bradley, Patti Standard— and another heart-stopping cowboy from Dorsey Kelley.

In the months to come, watch for Silhouette Romance novels by many more of your favorite authors, including Diana Palmer, Annette Broadrick, Elizabeth August and Marie Ferrarella.

The Silhouette authors and editors love to hear from readers, and we'd love to hear from *you*.

Happy reading from all of us at Silhouette!

Valerie Susan Hayward
Senior Editor

THE REAL MALLOY
Anne Peters

Silhouette
ROMANCE™
Published by Silhouette Books New York
America's Publisher of Contemporary Romance

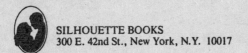

SILHOUETTE BOOKS
300 E. 42nd St., New York, N.Y. 10017

THE REAL MALLOY

Copyright © 1992 by Anne Hansen

ISBN: 0-373-08899-X

First Silhouette Books printing November 1992

Printed in the U.S.A.

Books by Anne Peters

Silhouette Romance

Through Thick and Thin #739
Next Stop: Marriage #803
And Daddy Makes Three #821
Storky Jones Is Back in Town #850
Nobody's Perfect #875
The Real Malloy #899

Silhouette Desire

Like Wildfire #497

ANNE PETERS

makes her home in the Pacific Northwest with her husband and their dog, Adrienne. Family and friends, reading, writing and travel—those are the things she loves most. Not always in that order, not always with equal fervor, but always without exception.

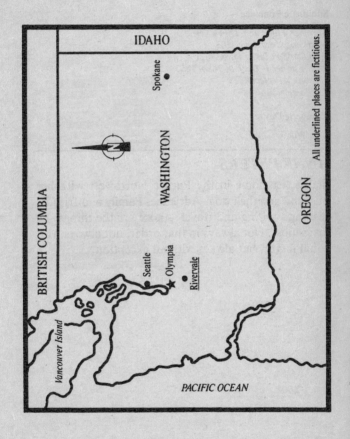

All underlined places are fictitious.

Prologue

"Oh, Bonnie, wait!"

"Can't." The young woman with the wire-rimmed glasses slowed neither her own pace nor the rapid trot of the little boy she was propelling up the hall. "Ricky's about to have an accident."

"Well, there's someone to see you. In my office."

"Be there in a jiff." Bonnie hustled her charge into the bathroom. "You promised to come tell me," she chided, tugging down the toddler's scruffy jeans and underpants as fast as she could.

"I did."

"Yeah, but *sooner*, Ricky. Or else," she added in hopes of providing further incentive, "your mom won't let you wear these awesome big-boy underpants again tomorrow."

Their mission accomplished, Bonnie briskly restored the little boy's modesty, praised him for re-

membering to flush and then for going to the sink to
have his hands washed. Now that Ricky's little crisis
had passed, she wondered who would come looking
for her here? Who besides Ellie Grimes and her family even knew she worked here?

"We made it," she told a motherly woman when she
and Ricky got back to the Toddler Room, "but Joan
wants me in her office."

"It's almost snack time."

"I know. And I'll be right back to help with them."

Standing outside of the Teeny Totters Day-care
Center's director's office, Bonnie wiped suddenly
damp palms on the seat of her faded jeans, then
scolded herself. What was there to be nervous about,
for Pete's sake? She hadn't done anything. On a deep
breath, she drew herself erect and knocked.

"Come in." A man's voice. Where was Joan?

Fighting renewed trepidation, Bonnie stepped into
the room, but only barely. She stayed near the door,
one hand holding it open to allow a quick exit should
it become necessary. She stared at the balding man
with his feet up on Joan's desk, took in the rumpled
suit and loosened tie, and her heart dropped into her
sneakers. Jeez—a cop. Reflex had her halfway out the
door.

"Hey!" There was a *thump* as the man's feet hit the
floor. "Wait. Miss Coombs?" And then he was beside her in the hall, making Bonnie wonder how a guy
with a paunch like that could move so fast. "You *are*
Bonanza Coombs?"

"Who wants to know?"

The question and Bonnie's undisguised hostility
made the man's eyebrows soar. "Jack Mercett," he

drawled. Drawing a billfold out of his pocket, he flipped it open and extended it to her.

Bonnie didn't spare it a glance. She warily kept her eyes on his. "You a cop?"

"Nope." With a shrug, Mercett snapped shut the billfold and stuffed it into his pocket. "Private investigator."

"So..." Some of the tension left Bonnie's body. "What do you want with me?"

"Just talk."

"About what?"

"Relax, kid. It's nothing bad." With a thin smile, Mercett gestured toward Joan's office. "Why'nt we go back inside?"

Bonnie didn't want to. In her book, private detectives ranked only a fraction higher than policemen. Snoops, all of them. And trouble.

"I'm clean," she said past the lump of terror in her throat, her voice tight. She had a regular job here. Thanks to Ellie, she finally had a life.

"I know that."

"I haven't done anything."

"Hey, it's okay," the man said, his tone unexpectedly kind. "Nobody's after you or anything, so like I said, relax. I've got some news for you. Good news." He went back into the office.

Reluctantly, Bonnie followed. As far as she was concerned, *no* news was the only good kind of news.

"Have a seat." Mercett had already planted himself behind the desk again.

"I'll stand."

"Suit yourself." He opened a worn briefcase and withdrew some papers. "Bonanza Loretta Coombs?" he asked formally, glancing up at her.

Bonnie swallowed. "Yeah."

"Your mother was Loretta Coombs of Euclid, Ohio?"

"Yes." The word came out grimly.

"Father, Roy Rogers Filmore of Rivervale, Washington?"

"I—" Bonnie bit her lip. Roy Rogers Filmore was a subject she didn't care to discuss.

Mercett glanced at her sharply. "Well?"

"Why are you asking me all these questions?"

"Just routine," the man said before repeating. "Well?"

Bonnie shrugged, her expression sullen. "I s'pose."

"You suppose *what?*"

"I s'pose the guy was my father."

The investigator sighed. "You're saying you're not sure?"

Mutely, Bonnie gave another pseudo-uncaring shrug.

"The birth records indicate—"

"Well, fine then," Bonnie snapped, as always mortified by the circumstances of her illegitimate birth. "If you already know all that, why're you asking me?"

"Just—"

"Routine. I know." Bonnie's lips twisted into a scornful grimace. "Yeah, well, I've got a roomful of toddlers to help feed so could we get to the point?"

"All right." Mercett heaved another sigh. "The point, Miss Coombs, is that your paternal grandmother, Addie Filmore, has spent considerable time and cash trying to track you down over the years. Seems you're the only child of her deceased son and she wanted you with her."

Bonnie stood statue still, uncomprehending, as she listened to Mercett's unemotional monologue.

"Unfortunately," he said, "she died before we were able to locate you. Three months ago, as a matter of fact, but before she went, she made you, Miss Coombs, the sole beneficiary of her estate and instructed me to keep looking for you."

He handed Bonnie a large manila envelope. "You'll find it's all in here."

Stunned, Bonnie dropped into the chair she had earlier disdained. Though her expression gave nothing away, inside she was devastated by the realization that she'd come *this* close to having a family, but had once again lost it.

She barely listened as Mercett proceeded to tell her the details.

Chapter One

Three months later

"So this is it, Bonanza. Rivervale, Washington."

"Really?" With a suddenly pounding heart, Bonnie leaned forward in the passenger seat of the aged and rusting station wagon. Squinting through the bug-spattered windshield, she saw ahead of her a long, tree-lined street flanked by single-story buildings. Stores, most of them, she surmised. And judging by the small number of people on the narrow sidewalks, none of them doing a heck of a lot of business. "I guess this is Main Street, huh?"

"I guess. If that sign over there is anything to go by."

Bonnie frowned at the street sign Eleanor Grimes indicated. "So which way do you s'pose Maple Street is from here?"

"Beats me." Gears grinding, Ellie slammed into first. "But in a town this size, how far away could it be?'' Proceeding through the intersection, the ancient car groaned and protested as it had most of the way from Los Angeles. ''Let's ask at that gas station over there.''

Content to let the older woman handle things, Bonnie took another long look around. So, she mused, her feelings mixed, this was Rivervale. They'd made it, and in just a few more minutes, she'd be at her house. At her very own home. The thought gave her both goose bumps and sweaty palms. She'd never really had a home in the sense that Ellie said this house was going to be. Even living the past couple of years at Ellie's place—though Ellie and her family had made Bonnie feel as welcome as could be—she'd always felt like a guest.

She was going to miss Ellie. Bonnie felt a surge of panic at the prospect of having to manage without her best friend. Ellie had been the anchor in her life for an awful long time now. Ever since Bonnie's days at the Whitworth Institute for Troubled Teens, Ellie had been there to scold, to help, to guide. To be cut loose from her now was scary, and again Bonnie wondered if she was really ready for this. Was she ready to stand on her own, to take responsibility for her life without anyone to turn to for advice? Without anyone to lean on except herself?

Maybe she should have taken the lawyer's advice after all and sold Addie Filmore's house.

Just as quickly as she had then, Bonnie dismissed that particular notion. She reminded herself of the promise she'd made to herself and to Ellie, the promise that from here on in, she would only look ahead. That she would take this gift she had been so miraculously given and use it to once and for all make a new beginning.

Imagine it. Bonnie hugged herself. A new beginning. All she'd ever known so far were endings. Bad ones, more often than not.

Ellie was rolling down her window and pulling into the service station. Warm, woodsy-smelling breezes mixed with the odor of gasoline wafted into the car. The gasoline part Bonnie recognized from L.A. The woodsy fragrance was a new experience, however. She liked it.

"What *is* that?" she asked, her nose twitching like a rabbit's. "That smell I smell . . ."

"Pines," Ellie replied, preoccupied with trying to locate someone to direct them.

As always, Bonnie was impressed by her friend's vast knowledge of just about everything.

"Or," Ellie absently mused, still looking around, "maybe cedars. One of those kinds of trees, anyway. Oh, excuse me!" She waved to one of the mechanics in the shop before adding to Bonnie, "This *is* the Evergreen State, you know."

Ellie smiled at the grease-smeared young man trotting over to their car. "Could you direct us to Maple Street, please?"

"Yes, ma'am. Straight ahead three blocks, then hang a left. Maple's the second road you'll come to."

"Thanks." Ellie glanced at the name stitched onto the attendant's work shirt pocket, and added, "Jimmy."

Bonnie marveled at and envied Ellie's easy way with people. She wished she had that kind of finesse.

"Who is it you're looking for?" Jimmy asked.

"Not who, what," said Ellie. "The Filmore house."

"Oh." Jimmy leaned closer. "You the grand-daughter?"

"Uh-uh." Ellie nodded toward Bonnie. "She is. Bonanza Coombs."

"Well, hi there!" Jimmy beamed a smile at Bonnie, his face hanging into the car almost upside down. "And welcome."

"Gee." Bonnie couldn't think of a thing to say. She couldn't remember ever having been welcomed any-place. Kicked out, yes... "Thanks...uh..."

"There, you see, what did I tell you?" Ellie said as they drove away. "Small-town people are friendly. You'll like it here."

Bonnie sincerely hoped so.

They had no trouble finding the place. Pulling up in front of the white, old-fashioned house with a roomy porch shading its front windows, Bonnie's heart slammed into her ribs. For the first time in fifteen years or more, she felt the sting of tears in her eyes. *Home,* she thought, buffeted by emotions too numer-ous and staggering to name. She looked at the scruffy lawn and overgrown shrubs and found them beauti-ful.

Afraid to betray the depth of her emotions, afraid the jinx that always seemed to be dogging her heels might snatch all this away, she said, "Not much, is it?"

Ellie rolled her eyes in mock exasperation. "You expected maybe the White House?"

"I mean, it's nice and all that..." Unbidden and unwelcome, tears clogged Bonnie's throat, making the words come out scratchy and hoarse. Her grandmother had lived here, she realized in a daze. The grandmother who had actually searched for her, who had thought of her and wanted her. And though they'd never met, this grandmother had cared about her enough to give her all this. It was all too much, and so Bonnie screwed up her face and tried to sound blasé. "In a middle-class, establishment kind of way. You know?"

"Oh, Bonnie, I do know." Turning, Ellie gave her a fierce hug. "And not only do I think it's wonderful, I think it's great. Especially since it's all yours."

"Yes." With burning eyes Bonnie stared at the house. "It's all mine." And suddenly she was flooded with so much happiness, she wanted to jump up and down, dance, anything. What she did, though, was grin foolishly at Ellie through a veil of unshed tears. "It really is, isn't it?"

"You betcha." Ellie cleared her throat and fixed her young friend with a stern look. "Signed and delivered to you by someone who loved you, Bonanza. I want you to remember that next time the lonelies grab hold of you."

"I'll try."

"See that you do. This is your chance to start over, Bon. With a house of your own and twenty-five thousand dollars after taxes. Remember, you've got goals now, so make it all work for you, you hear?"

Make it all work.

Roused from her bed a week later, at eleven o'clock at night, by a black-haired, tough-looking individual who insisted he was her upstairs tenant, Bonnie wasn't so sure she could. She *was* sure, however, that she appreciated neither the quick once-over the man gave her nor his subsequent unimpressed dismissal. And she'd be damned if she'd just willy-nilly let him come in. She told him so.

Whereupon he said, "Look, kid," in the kind of tone Bonnie used to use in dealing with the toddlers at the day care, "why don't you run in and get your mother, all right? Not that I blame you for being careful and questioning me—I don't—but it's been a long day and I'd just as soon talk with whoever's in charge."

"I'm—" Assertive, not belligerent, Bonanza, Ellie's voice inside her head remonstrated. On a deep breath, Bonnie moderated her tone. "I am in charge."

"You're kidding." This time the man's inspection was narrow eyed, thorough and openly skeptical. *"You're* Addie Filmore's granddaughter?"

"I am."

"And you said your name was...what?" Suspicion laced his drawl.

"I didn't say." Bonnie tried manfully to outstare the man, though inside she quivered like jelly and fiercely wished Ellie could have stuck around just one more day to handle this. "I'd like to hear yours, though."

"Would you now?" He subjected Bonnie to another assessing stare before, apparently convinced she was who she said she was, he gave her his name. "Malloy. Frank Malloy."

Damn. Bonnie winced inwardly. Malloy was the name the lawyer had mentioned, but somehow she'd created the image of an older, and...well, nicer man in her head. Disappointment made her tighten her grip on the door. "So if you live here, how come you don't have a key?"

"I've been trying to tell you—" Malloy's frown matched the impatient tone it accompanied. "I've been on a hunting trip..."

That explained his scruffy condition, Bonnie supposed.

"...and I put the key under that flowerpot over there so I wouldn't lose it. I've done it for years, but this time, it's gone."

"I know." Feeling superior in the face of such stupidity, Bonnie crossed her arms and sharpened her expression. "I took it."

"You...?"

"It's a dumb place to leave a key. It's the first place they look."

"They?"

"Thieves, burglars."

"Ah." Malloy nodded. "Firsthand knowledge?"

His sarcasm grated. Bonnie's chin came up. "Maybe."

"I see." For reasons Bonnie couldn't fathom but which nevertheless annoyed her no end, he seemed to find her reply amusing. His lips twitched. "So can I come in?"

Bonnie didn't budge. "You got ID?"

Rolling his eyes, Malloy dragged a slim folder out of his back pocket. "My driver's license." He held it out to her. "See? This address is on it and everything."

Bonnie squinted down at it. The photo wasn't the best, but it was undeniably him. Unable to think of any other objections, she capitulated. "Okay, you can come in." She stepped back into the entry and reached for the key on the hook beside the front door. A little gingerly, she gave it to him. "But I'm coming upstairs with you."

She was entitled, she assured herself in answer to the sardonic glance he shot her as he shouldered past. She was, after all, the landlady here. Another thought occurred to her, and she quickly gave it voice. "And I want to see the lease."

She figured that if he could come up with a convincing looking piece of paper, she would accept the inevitable—at least until she could figure out some way to kick him out. Apart from the fact that goodlooking, macho types like Malloy were a pain in the a—*Watch your language, Bonanza.* Ellie's voice intruded again—were a pain in the neck, there was something about this guy that made Bonnie nervous. It was something she couldn't quite put her finger on, but it was there. Once again she wished Ellie were, too.

The steep flight of stairs leading to Malloy's attic apartment ran straight up from the front door. Climbing them in the man's wake, keeping her eyes down after one unintentional and disturbing glance at muscular buttocks in faded jeans, Bonnie reminded herself that she was in charge. This was her house; she was the landlady. She had the power here, not he.

She straightened her shoulders and stiffened her spine. And bumped—smack—into Malloy's broad back. He had stopped on the narrow landing to unlock the door, but he hadn't opened it.

"Sorry." Bonnie took a hasty back and downward step. "What's the matter?"

"I don't let anybody in whose name I don't know."

"Oh." Just like that, Bonnie felt foolish again, gauche. She should've introduced herself by now— Ellie would have. Frowning, she averted her eyes from Malloy's startlingly dark blue gaze. "I, uh, I'm Bonanza."

Kids used to laugh when she told them that, adults sometimes smirked. They asked how she liked riding the range or where her horse was. She'd quickly grown tired of those jokes. Somebody or other once told her the word—her name—meant "windfall." But the meaning of *that* word had eluded her, too, until one day she'd finally asked Ellie about it. *Windfall* meant sudden good fortune, Ellie had explained. And Bonnie, remembering the circumstances of her birth, as well as her mother's general attitude, had thought *that* was funny!

She slanted Malloy a look to catch his reaction to her funny name and saw him eyeing her thoughtfully. "Yeah," he said, "I remember now. Bonanza Coombs. Addie'd call you Bonnie, though, when she talked about you to me."

Bonnie's breath caught. "She talked about me?"

"Sure did. Quite often." The corner of his eyes crinkled, settling into the lines already there. "For some reason, I thought you'd be older."

"I thought the same about you."

For the first time since Bonnie had opened the door to Malloy's impatient ringing, they regarded each other with something like friendliness. Malloy smiled, and Bonnie, thinking maybe he wasn't so bad after all, smiled back.

"Well." He pushed open the door, reached in to flip on a light and gestured with his hand. "Go in, then."

Curious and still smiling, Bonnie stepped into a tiny living room. She cast a quick look around at tasteful, contemporary furnishings and shelves of books, and then she sneezed. Rapidly, twice, three times. Four and five...

"Cats!" Horrified and still hachooing, she spun toward Malloy who had come in behind her. "You've got cats!"

"Only one," he assured her. "His name is Sam, and he's boarded out right now."

"I don't care." Eyes streaming, Bonnie sneezed yet again. Groping in her bathrobe's pockets for a tissue, she found none. Ungraciously she accepted the one Malloy was holding out to her. "I'm sorry," she stated flatly after she'd blown her nose and wiped her eyes, "but there's no way that cat can stay. He has got to go."

"Go? This is the only home Sam knows—"

"I don't care." *Ha-chooooo!* "I'm giving Sam—or you and Sam, take your pick—notice. And that's final."

"And I'm telling you you can't do that—"

"Oh, can't I?" Malloy had no way of knowing it, of course, but telling Bonanza "you can't" was like waving a red flag in front of a bull: she invariably charged full steam ahead. "Watch me," she said, yanking the key out of the doorlock and pocketing it with a so-there expression. "Be packed up and out of here by tomorrow night, Malloy."

"Whoa! Just a minute!" Tight-lipped, Malloy strode to a bureau, pulled open a drawer and extracted a sheet of paper. "The lease you mentioned." He waved it in front of her.

"Let me see that."

"My pleasure." He handed it over with a flourish.

Nervously chewing her lower lip, Bonnie stared at the document. It looked official enough. Damn.

"I think it'll read better this way." Deadpan, Malloy reached out and turned the paper a hundred eighty degrees.

Crimson heat stained Bonnie's cheek. "I, uh, I don't see too good without my glasses." Fiercely scowling, she thrust the lease back at him. "Just tell me when it runs out, all right?"

"Sure." His eyes gleamed. "How does December thirty-first grab you?"

"December? But that's—" Bonnie rapidly calculated. "That's six, almost seven months away!"

"Life's a bitch, ain't it?" He held out his hand. "My key?"

"Not so fast. How do I know you're not lying?"

For a long moment he only glared at her, audibly drawing breath through flared nostrils. She'd gotten to him with that one, Bonnie surmised a bit uncomfortably. But, damn it all, he was being deliberately difficult and—

"I'll be glad to wait while you run downstairs to get your glasses so you can read the lease for yourself," he finally suggested in acid tones.

Oh. That *would* fix it, wouldn't it? The unwelcome logic of his suggestion once again forced Bonnie to capitulate. "No, that's okay. I guess I believe you."

"Gee, thanks."

Ignoring his sarcasm, she handed back his key. "You're being very hard-nosed about this, Malloy. I happen to be *allergic* to cats, you know...."

"Yeah. And I'm allergic to people who try to throw their weight around, so tell you what—" He strode to the door and yanked it open. "You stay in your part of the house, and I'll stay in mine and maybe neither of us'll have a problem."

Standing in his doorway on top of the stairs and watching Bonanza Coombs descend them in a stiff-shouldered huff, Frank frowned at the notion that *this* was his new landlady. Good Lord, she was little more than a kid! She didn't fit his expectations in the least— not that he'd thought about it all that much.

Addie used to talk to him about the kind of woman she imagined her granddaughter had grown up to be. For just an instant, Frank wondered if she'd have been as annoyed with Bonanza's attitude about Sam as he was, but then he decided it didn't matter. What mattered was that Sam belonged in this house every bit as much as Bonanza Coombs did, if not more. After all, the cat had been Addie's faithful companion for many years, besides which, Frank had promised her he'd see to it Sam would always be taken care of.

All of which he'd gladly have explained to that half-baked new landlady of his if she hadn't gone off half-cocked and threatened him with eviction.

Frank's lips twisted as he shook his head. He'd bet that young woman had been hell on wheels as a kid, the way she reacted when she thought herself challenged. She had a temper on her, that was for sure, but there was something else, too. A wariness, an uncertainty that she strove to disguise with bluster. In his line of work, he came across similar attitudes all the time, in kids on the street who shouldn't be; in young hoodlums and troublemakers.

He watched her stiffly round the newel post at the bottom of the stairs, saw her slant him a fulminating glare in the process. And it occurred to him to wonder just exactly where Bonanza Coombs might have been all those years Addie searched and couldn't find her.

Did he care enough to do some checking?

Chapter Two

Six months to go on the lease, Malloy had said.

The minute Bonnie had gotten downstairs after her tenant had so rudely shown her the door, she had flipped six pages of her calendar and circled the month of December in red. And afterward she'd promised herself that for those long and miserable six months ahead, she'd ignore both man and cat as much as possible.

Which so far, in the man's case, hadn't been easy, because whenever Malloy was home, she'd swear all he did was march around in hiking boots. His floors—her *ceilings*—creaked and groaned as he did whatever it was he did, and all that racket made it impossible to shut him out.

The cat, on the other hand, had not been a problem so far. Except that for some reason, he tried to come into *her* part of the house whenever she opened the front or back door. Though he made her sneeze, Bonnie had nothing against Sam personally or against cats in general, for that matter. In fact, she liked them much better than dogs, whose dispositions tended to remind her of her mother's: no matter what some guy dished out, she took it and pretty much begged for more, and all the while she snarled and attacked her own kind just like dog bitches did.

Not that Bonnie had really thought about it in those exact terms before, but observing Sam the cat's regal comings and goings brought home to Bonnie the fact that cats'd be the species worth emulating. Cats were independent creatures, and they bestowed as well as accepted attachments and affection strictly on their own terms—just as Bonnie was determined to do.

Closing the door in his face yet again and watching Sam's disdainful departure, Bonnie felt a wave of almost affection toward the animal. Just look at the way he waved that fat white tail in the air, proud and straight, like the flag of a conquering army. He was leaving because he wanted to, it seemed to say, not because he couldn't have snuck past her if he'd really tried.

With his back to her, he sat down on the porch railing to wash before going on about his business. He was a handsome calico, all yellow and white, and he came and went to *his* part of the house by way of the outside stairs in back, which led to a little deck off Malloy's kitchenette.

Bonnie knew this because she had crept up there one day when Malloy was gone. Feeling ridiculously like a sneak—this was her house, after all—she had peeked into both sets of his windows. Through the one she'd seen the kitchen: a tiny refrigerator, a standard sink-and-stove sort of arrangement, a bowl of fruit on a square white table with two chairs. Through the other windows, one of which was partially open to allow Sam entry and exit, she'd looked into Malloy's bedroom. A navy blue, cream-and-taupe-patterned spread covered a bed, the size of which had reminded her that he might well be inclined to bring female companions home with him from time to time. Or even regularly.

How did she feel about that? She didn't. Not only that, she resolved that for a matter of only six months, she wouldn't. It—he—was nothing to her.

Overall, the man kept his apartment tidy. Bonnie supposed she had to be grateful for that. She further supposed that as renters went, she really could have done worse—though she'd prefer him some thirty years older, less attractive and without a cat.

Old Mrs. Savage from next door had caught sight of Bonnie at Malloy's windows and had eyed her *very* peculiarly. Still they had exchanged smiles and stilted introductions, which was more than Bonnie had done so far with anyone else in town. Contrary to what Ellie had said, of the people in Rivervale she'd come in contact with—by choice admittedly few—only Florence Jackson, the checkout clerk at Miller's market, greeted and treated Bonnie with any degree of warmth.

Still, Bonnie was happy in her new home. After years of never belonging anywhere, she was determined to *belong* in Rivervale. Or at least in this house. She didn't mind being alone—the need for privacy, for her own inviolate space, had been an almost physical hunger for as long as she could remember. She didn't even mind the rainy weather and the chill that came with it, in spite of it being late May. She simply invested in several big sweatshirts to layer over the T-shirts she liked to wear with her jeans, and that was that.

Except today she was totally chilled to the bone. Laying down the charcoal with which she'd been trying to sketch, Bonnie blew into her hands. A shiver raced up and down her back and arms, puckering the skin. She should turn on the furnace, she thought. She knew there was one in the basement, a potbellied monstrosity made from sheet metal or some such material. What she didn't know was how to activate the thing.

Would Malloy?

He was home. She could hear him, or rather, she could hear his music. Whatever he was listening to was all bass and reverberated through her ceiling with a rhythmic *thump, thump, thump.* They hadn't spoken since that first night eight days ago. And, to be honest, she'd just as soon not go up there and speak to him now. She especially hated having to ask him for a favor. But on the other hand, she was freezing, so who else was there?

When faced with a dilemma, don't just toss common sense to the wind and charge.

Bonnie could hear Ellie's lecture, the one that decried Bonnie's habit of acting first and thinking later, as if her friend were in the room with her right this very minute.

You've got a good brain, Bonanza, use it. People have choices.

No, they don't. I never did.

*They do and you did. Only you were too pigheaded
and hurt to know it most of the time. Always weigh
your options, Bonanza....*

Her options.

All right, she would weigh them. One: If she did
nothing, pretty soon her fingers would freeze and
eventually fall off. In which case she wouldn't be able
to feed herself or paint, and she'd probably die. Two:
Again, if she did nothing, she could conceivably catch
a chill that would escalate into pneumonia. She'd take
to her bed, unable to get up and feed herself or paint
and, again, curtains. Three: She could swallow her
pride, go upstairs and ask Malloy to help her. He'd be
rude and refuse, which would make her so mad, she'd
kill him.

Three it was.

The music got louder with each increasingly halt-
ing step Bonnie took up the stairs. She had to knock
several times, hard, before there was a response. Then,
however, the door practically flew off its hinges, and
Bonnie could only stand there and stare because, except for the skimpy towel riding low on his hips, Frank
Malloy was naked, dripping—and gorgeous.

So that's what Greek gods looked like in the flesh!

Bonnie reared back. She'd never admit it out loud,
of course, but the truth was she felt thoroughly intimidated by so much masculine virility at close range.
Frank Malloy was all muscle and lean, with not an
ounce of fat anywhere to spoil the clean definition and
downright—there was no other word for it—*beauty* of
his physique.

Bonnie wanted to paint him more than she had ever wanted anything, but she doubted she'd be good enough to do him justice in the unlikely event he would agree to pose for her in the even more unlikely event she was crazy enough to ask him.

"What?" Frank didn't bother to hide his displeasure at having his shower interrupted. Bonanza stood mute, staring, causing Frank to grip his towel to make sure it hadn't slipped. "What's the matter? Music too loud?"

"What? Oh. No." Get a hold of yourself, Bonnie Coombs. "I, umm, I was cold, and I wondered..." She faltered, her eyes now fixed on some spot on the wall next to her. Malloy's impatience was a palpable thing, and she nervously cleared her throat.

He spoke before she finally could. "Wondered *what?*"

His testy tone made Bonnie mad enough to overcome the attack of nerves. Hadn't she known he'd be rude?

Her head snapped around, and her chin jerked up. "Forget it, okay?" She spun on her heel and started back down the stairs.

"Hold it." The hand Frank clamped on her shoulder was not gentle. God, she was skinny. Instantly his grip relaxed. Angry gazes clashed. "Don't you dare drag me out of the shower just so you can have an audience for your temper tantrum."

"Ha!" Bonnie tossed her head. "*I'm* not the one with the tantrum."

Frank ignored that. He narrowed his eyes. "You said you were cold," he reiterated with menacing softness, "and you wondered. After which I asked you what it was you were wondering. Now I'll ask you just one more time. What is it?''

Bonnie sniffed. She shrugged off his hand, but some hint of authority in his voice forced her to respond with a measure of civility she sorely begrudged him. "It's the furnace," she said. "I wondered if you could maybe show me how to turn it on."

She had come to him for help and, frowning at her in consternation as he was, Frank could tell it had cost her.

"All right." He sucked in a deep breath to release the tension her attitude had caused. "Sure. I'd, uh, be glad to."

"T-thanks." A smile accompanied his negligent shrug, and Bonnie quickly averted her eyes again. Her heart beat faster, suddenly, and she knew an urge to bolt down the stairs. She forced herself to stay where she was, but kept her eyes lowered. "Thanks a lot."

"No problem." Since he'd obviously upset her a minute ago with his bark, Frank forced a lighter tone. Hell, she was Addie's granddaughter. He ought to take it easy with her. "Look, I'll be there in a minute, all right? Unless you want to come in and wait? Heat rises, you know. It's warm in here...."

"No, that's okay." This time Bonnie did bolt, and she could swear she'd heard him chuckle before he closed the door. Egotistical jerk, she fumed, red-faced and annoyed with herself. He probably thought he was God's gift to women or something. And no wonder, the way she'd stared. Jeez...

It seemed much less than the minute Malloy had mentioned when he rapped on the kitchen door and stepped through it. He had put on baggy, gray sweats, but his feet were bare and his hair was still wet. Here and there the sweats clung damply, making Bonnie realize that he hadn't bothered to towel himself dry before jumping into some clothes and coming to her aid.

The observation made her soften toward him, but it also made her uncomfortable and self-conscious all over again. All the more so because, suddenly, he struck her as extremely sexy, where earlier, upstairs, she'd mostly been impressed by the aesthetic beauty of him, as well as intimidated by his obvious physical strength. To be honest, she'd have preferred to hang on to those earlier feelings....

She saw him glance around as he crossed the kitchen toward where she stood by the basement door and, anxious to fill what seemed to her a heavy silence, she said, "Nothing's changed. My grandmother—"

How odd that word sounded, coming out of her mouth. Saying it made her feel like an impostor. After all, for all she'd left Bonnie her house and money, Addie Filmore was still a stranger.

And so Bonnie said, "Addie Filmore willed all her stuff to me along with the house. I haven't had time to, you know, change anything...."

"Sure."

As if he cares, dum-dum.

Bonnie hurried herself down the basement stairs, feeling foolish for rambling on and, even more, for being so damn aware of his presence right behind her. Still, she was glad he was there, because she didn't like the dark and, except for the triangle of light from the open kitchen door, it was black as coal below. She'd noticed the other day that the cellar's two small windows had boards nailed over them on the outside. Maybe Addie had been afraid of burglars getting into the house that way or something.

Personally, Bonnie feared burglars less than dark places and so she stopped on the bottom step to fumble for the string hanging from the naked bulb overhead. She almost fell flat on her face as her sudden stop had Frank Malloy crashing into her. Only his hands firmly gripping her shoulders kept her from pitching forward.

"Whoa, there." For the second time in less than ten minutes Frank was struck by Bonanza Coombs's fragility. Her shoulder bones felt as if he could crush them without any effort at all. And for just an instant he was touched yet again by the elusive air of defenselessness he'd sensed about her before. This new landlady of his might come across as tough, but he'd been trained to look beyond the fronts people put up.

Consequently, he was pretty sure Bonanza Coombs was no tougher than most of the other scared-to-death juvenile delinquents he'd steered back onto the straight and narrow in his time. What was more, he was increasingly convinced she'd once been one of their number.

Steadying her, he remembered last week's fleeting intention to check out her past. He'd forgotten about it till now, had forgotten how he'd been puzzled by her then, too. She seemed to be such a contradiction in personalities—at once brazen and bashful, testy and timid, iniquitous and innocent. Vexatious, as often as not, and yet so seemingly vulnerable.

"You okay?" Acutely aware, suddenly, of the slender back he was all but pressing against his lower body, Frank released her.

"I'm fine." The instant Frank withdrew his hands, Bonnie leapt down the last couple of steps to the floor. Her back burned from the feel of him, her cheeks with reaction to his touch and smell. He had smelled of soap and cleanliness, and he'd felt so solid and warm against her back. Could she really have been cold earlier?

Frank yanked the string and flooded the room with light. Bonnie stood facing toward him, and he was struck again by how incredibly young she looked. Without makeup and with plenty of freckles across her tip-tilted nose, she looked barely sixteen, though logic told him that she had to be older.

"Just how old are you, anyway?" he blurted.

"Twenty-one. Why?"

She sounded wary again, suspicious. What was it with her? He resolved to find out, but now only shrugged. "Just wondered. You look very young."

"So you've said before."

"Well, it's true." Frank told himself he had no reason to be on the defensive, but her wary attitude put him there just the same. It was ridiculous. What did she think he wanted with her? With a deep breath to bank his escalating temper, he walked past her to the furnace and hunkered down in front of it.

"There's a little thingamajig here that you press and hold," he curtly informed her, glancing up with frowning impatience when she continued to just stand where she was. "Look, if you need your glasses on for this, better go get 'em. I don't have all day."

Her glasses. Bonnie touched her face. She'd taken them off to sketch since they always slid down her nose.

"That's okay." She came to kneel beside him, stiffly, and giving off almost palpable vibrations of injured pride as she said, "I don't think I'll need 'em."

Touchy. With a sigh, Frank forced himself once again to moderate his tone. "Whatever you say. I guess this gets done mostly by touch anyhow. Here, give me your hand." Taking hold of the fingers she extended, he guided one of them into the furnace and onto a little knob. "Feel that?"

Bonnie nodded, feeling much more than just the button. She felt the press of Malloy's thigh, his arm, his fingers and the warmth of his breath on her cheek as he spoke. She felt her heartbeat pick up speed and her mouth go dry.

And in the face of Frank Malloy's obvious detachment, she felt ticked off with herself for reacting to him as she did.

Jiminy! Was she so starved for human contact that all it took to set her off was the incidental touch of a man who was merely being neighborly? Was she that lonely?

"You got a match on you?" Frank asked. Bonanza Coombs's hand, so small in his, was trembling, he noted. Because he knew a crazy urge to keep hold of it, he let it go and sat back on his heel. "See," he said with careful casualness, "pressing that gizmo the way you're doing is making the gas come down. So now all you have to do is touch a match to the spot and, bingo, your pilot light's lit."

"I don't have a match." Bonnie, too, straightened. No use pressing the button when she had nothing to light the gas with.

"At all?"

"Well I don't know. I don't smoke anymore—" She broke off, flushing, and with a quick glance at him, scrambled to her feet. "What I mean is—"

"Glad you gave it up." Frank had a pretty good idea what she'd meant. "Nasty habit." He, too, straightened from his crouch. "I bet Addie has matches in a drawer somewhere. That woman was prepared for anything, I swear."

"What was she like?" The question was out before Bonnie knew she'd even thought it.

"Addie?" Frank, one foot already on the stairs, stopped to look back. "She was a nice lady. Well thought of in this town. A heart of gold. I guess you've seen pictures of her in her stuff upstairs, so I don't need to tell you what she looked like. She looked good, though, I always thought. Handsome, I guess the word is. She had an air about her, stately, and she kept to herself a lot. More so after her son got killed, I've been told. I never really knew him very well—your father...."

"I didn't, either," Bonnie said quietly.

Their eyes met. Frank's gaze was full of sympathy.

Bonnie hated that. "No big deal." She shoved her hands into her jeans pockets and tossed off a stiff-armed shrug. "I mean, I'll bet lots of people don't know their relatives, right?"

As it happened, Frank knew all of his relatives. Except for his Grandmother Shaughnessy, but he'd heard so much about her that he felt as if he knew her, too. Most of the Shaughnessy and Malloy gang lived within a hundred-mile radius of Rivervale, and a good many of them were right here in town.

Frank had grown up here; he'd been a jock at Rivervale High, playing both football and basketball at varsity level. Which might not be impressive to some big-city high schooler, but it had made him a pretty big fish in his own little pond.

It could also have gotten him an athletic scholarship into one of the universities in the state, but all he'd ever wanted to be was a policeman. Just like his father and grandfather had been. And so he'd gone to community college for a couple of years, taking law-enforcement courses, and later he'd gotten into the State Patrol Academy.

He'd served on the patrol for several years, but had returned to Rivervale and joined the force there when his pop retired. He liked the slower pace and he liked the idea of having a hand in keeping his hometown a place where kids could grow up in relative safety. He hoped to have kids of his own someday, if ever he found the right kind of woman to marry and have them with.

His mother thought his problem was he was just too picky. She took every opportunity to tell him so. So did she think he should settle for just anybody, for crying out loud? Frank suspected that at this point, she did, the way she kept pushing any and all eligible females in his direction.

Today, though, Darlene Malloy wasn't pushing. On the contrary, she was eyeing her son sternly while, at the same time, pressing more meat loaf on Frank, Senior.

"People are talking, Junior," she said. "They're wondering if it's a good idea, you living in a house with a single woman the way you do."

Frank calmly ladled gravy over his mashed potatoes. "Addie Filmore was a single woman, too, Mom," he said with a wink at his father, who hid his grin behind a forkful of food. "I don't recall anybody talking and wondering about that."

"You know what I mean." His mother handed him the peas and carrots. "And they say she's from California, too."

"Oh, my." Another wink, man-to-man, passed across the table. "Now that *is* awful, isn't it?"

"Go ahead, laugh." Darlene gave a sniff and an injured toss of the head. "You'll do what you want anyway, I suppose."

"I'm thirty years old, Mom."

"Don't meddle, Darlene," the elder Frank admonished his wife. "Give the boy some credit. After all, it's not like he's sharing a room with the woman or anything. He's got his own apartment, just like always. Bet you hardly ever see her, do you, Junior?"

Frank speared a chunk of meat loaf and shrugged. "I see her."

Truth and trouble was, he "saw" Bonnie even when he didn't. Meaning she was on his mind more often than she ought to be.

After lighting her furnace the other day, she had barely thanked him before she'd rushed into what used to be Addie's guest bedroom and slammed the door. She'd been upset. Something to do with what they'd been talking about, no doubt—her father. Frank didn't need to be a police detective to arrive at that conclusion.

Ever since, though, he'd been fracturing his brain trying to remember what all Addie had told him about Roy Rogers Filmore. It came to him in pieces. Like the fact that Addie's husband, the very late Marvin Filmore—he'd died shortly after young Roy's birth—had had a thing for Western movies in general and Roy Rogers in particular.

Another day he remembered Addie confiding that her son had been a traveling salesman and that she'd had him late in life. Roy married late, too, and moved to Portland, Oregon. Something about his not having any kids—with the wife, anyway. There'd been a waitress in Euclid, Ohio, however, with whom good old Roy had had a lengthy—and obviously fruitful—affair. Bonanza's mother.

Frank seemed to recall Addie saying there'd been talk of adoption. Apparently, though, not only had the wife balked at the notion, but the child's mother had, too. Roy and his wife had been killed in an accident before a resolution could be reached.

And so, in one tragic moment, Addie had lost both her son, and the chance to know her only grandchild.

Thinking back on the telling of it, Frank was struck by the realization that Addie seemed to have mourned the latter much more than the former. And he wondered if maybe she'd recognized mistakes she'd made in raising her son. Had she hoped to atone for those mistakes by taking care of her grandchild?

Frank didn't know, of course. What he did know, however, was that he'd cared very much for old Addie. And that even though on the surface Bonanza Coombs was nothing at all like her grandmother, he had a strong hunch that underneath, she was everything Addie had been . . . and more.

He knew he was probably crazy to not just let it go, and even crazier for letting Bonnie Coombs get under his skin the way he had, but he couldn't let it rest. He just *had* to find out what that "more" he sensed about her was.

Chapter Three

Learning that Bonanza Coombs seemed to be *less* rather than *more* like Addie Filmore came as a shock. Or was it, Frank brooded, unfair of him to make judgments about the facts he'd electronically brought to life with the aid of the department's computer? Was he wrong to feel those facts diminished Bonnie in some way?

At odds with himself, he pinched the bridge of his nose between thumb and forefinger, and closed his eyes. So she had a record. So what? Glumly, he stared at the computer screen once again.

It was juvenile stuff. A bunch of misdemeanors, that's all. Shoplifting, truancy, vagrancy. That sort of thing. It seemed Bonanza Coombs had been a chronic runaway from numerous foster homes before they'd slammed her into Whitworth at age fourteen. She'd been rebellious there, too, a handful, a troublemaker. But she'd stuck it out.

According to the record, she'd been clean ever since. There was nothing, not even a parking ticket. Not that that should be surprising, given the fact that nowhere did it say the woman had ever had a driver's license, much less a car. A quick check with the California DMV verified the quite astounding fact that Bonanza Coombs was one of those rare people in the U.S. of A. who didn't drive.

Rocking his chair onto its two hind legs, Frank contemplated that particularly surprising discovery with pursed lips, but in the end he was forced to grimly concede that neither the streets nor the Whitworth Institute had been environments conducive to automobile ownership.

So where, he now asked himself, had his colorful landlady spent her time after her release from reform school? Where had she been found?

Mercett.

With a *thump*, Frank's chair landed back on all fours. Now why hadn't he thought of that sooner? Jack Mercett was the investigator Addie had hired to track down her granddaughter. Frank, himself, had given her the name. He'd known Mercett from his state patrol days.

In moments Frank had Mercett on the line, and in another few moments after that, he was in possession of a couple more pieces of the puzzle named Bonanza Coombs. It seemed she had worked at the Teeny Totters Day-care Center in Los Angeles as a helper, and had resided in the home of one Eleanor Grimes, who was also the party responsible for getting Bonanza the job.

Eleanor Grimes. Frank pondered the name, wondering why it had a familiar ring to it. A few rapid keystrokes solved that riddle, too. Eleanor Grimes had been Bonanza's counselor at Whitworth. She was a social worker....

Driven by a need to know all there was to know about Bonnie, a need he would have been hard put to find the words to explain, Frank tapped out yet another series of telephone numbers until he'd at last tracked down Eleanor Grimes. But it wasn't until Frank heard a preoccupied female voice murmur "Hello?" that it occurred to him to wonder precisely what it was he wanted to ask the woman.

When had the cold facts about Bonanza Coombs ceased to be the only things of interest to him? When had it become important to know what her life—her everyday days—had been like? To know what it was that had driven her from foster home to foster home? And to know what it was that had driven her away from her mother?

Frank had no answer to those questions, he knew only that he needed to know. That he wanted to understand. That he wanted—what?

At a loss, he sought refuge in officialdom. "Ah. Mrs. Grimes?"

"Yes?"

Her impatience did nothing to calm Frank's rattled nerves. "This, uh..." He floundered, cleared his throat and began again. "This is Detective Sergeant Frank Malloy of the Rivervale, Washington police...."

"Oh . . . ?"

The woman's now wary tone alerted Frank to the fact that she might well misconstrue the nature of this call. "It's about Bonanza Coombs," he hastened to add, "but it's—" He paused again, frowning. Just what the hell *was* the nature of this call? How and why had he ever gotten himself into this?

Eleanor Grimes obviously wondered, too. More, she seemed none too pleased, if her sharply issued "Yes?" was anything to go by.

"It's, uh, actually, it's unofficial," Frank finished lamely. He felt like a bumbling rookie confronted with a hostile witness. "I just wanted to ask you a few questions about her."

"Really?" He could fairly hear the woman bristling. "For what reason?"

"Strictly personal," Frank assured her, rubbing a hand across his forehead and finding sweat there. "I just wondered... Ms. Coombs is my landlady. I knew her grandmother pretty well. I, uh, I checked Bonnie out on the computer...."

"I see." Arctic cold crept through the wires to chill him. "And you discovered that Bonanza has a record, is that it?"

"Well, yeah. Though, to tell you the truth, I had a hunch—"

"How astute of you," Ellie Grimes said frostily. "So what do you want from me?"

"I just want you to tell me about her. She lived with you. You know her pretty well—"

"And I'm her *friend,* Officer Malloy."

"So am I. Or at least I'd like to be."

"After you find out if she's worthy, is that it?"

"No!" Yet even as he angrily barked the denial, Frank felt himself guiltily flushing. And a tiny voice inside him sneered, *Liar!*

Eleanor Grimes's derisive laugh underscored the epithet even as she dismissed his objection with a brisk "Whatever." After which she said, "I'm afraid you've come to the wrong person, Officer Malloy. Bonnie's past is her own. It's hers to share or not to share, not mine. I suggest that if you really want to be her friend, you get to know the wonderful person she's become instead of snooping into the misfortunes of her youth and childhood looking for dirt—"

"I wasn't snooping," Frank protested. "And I'm certainly not looking for dirt."

"Aren't you? Then just what *are* you doing?"

Hadn't he been asking himself the same things? Frank fidgeted. "Why, I—"

"Does Bonanza know you're a cop, Officer Malloy?"

"Well—" Did she? They had never talked about his job in so many words. "What's that got to do with anything?"

"Now *that* I'll be glad to tell you, Officer Malloy. Bonnie has a thing about cops. She doesn't like them, and she doesn't trust them. Call it an unfortunate but understandable legacy of her past. Whatever. The bottom line is, as a cop—" She gave a scornful little laugh. "You want to be her friend? Mister, you're starting out with three strikes against you even without all this snooping you're doing."

"Now look here, lady. I told you—"

"And I'm telling you. Look, has Bonanza broken any laws?"

"No. Of course not."

"Then no matter what you say, officer, what you're doing is snooping. Worse, you're abusing your position of trust as a public servant, not to mention that you're blatantly invading a citizen's right to privacy—"

"Now, just a damn minute, Mrs. Grimes—"

"I'm afraid I can't spare you even that much more of my time, Officer Malloy. Good*bye!*"

Slack-jawed and feeling uncomfortably like a ten-year-old whose ears had just been blistered by one of the sisters in Sunday school, Frank stared at the receiver in his hand. Then, with a curse, he slammed the thing down, snapped off the computer and scraped back his chair.

Damn it to hell, he thought, surging to his feet. All he wanted was a little information. Him, snooping? Ridiculous!

He kicked the chair and it shot into place beneath his desk. He slapped the wall and glared at the Ponderosa pine outside of his window. A few innocent questions, a few illuminating answers, that's all he'd been after. Right?

Turning, Frank sighed. Yeah, right. So how come he felt like such a sleazeball?

Ignoring the stares from his colleagues, Frank stalked out of the station and headed for the only place in town that could possibly make him feel better about himself just then—Saint Christopher's Shelter and Mission. With luck he'd be able to scare up some kids to shoot a few baskets, even though this wasn't Wednesday, the day he regularly volunteered at Saint C's. He was the mission's athletic coach and—Frank grimaced, still smarting from Eleanor Grimes's pithy assessment of him—the all-around positive male role model for the assorted youngsters who, in addition to battered wives and indigent strays, were housed at the shelter at any given time.

Tossing a wave at Father Joseph MacAllister through the open door of the director's office, Frank's stride abruptly slowed at the sight of a familiar set of bony shoulders brushed by a brown fall of straight, shiny hair.

Bonanza Coombs, the very last person he wanted to come face-to-face with just then, was sitting across from Father Joe.

Frank hurried past the office door, his face now averted. And he wondered what Bonnie was doing there.

Bonnie was chasing the cat.

She'd been painting in the studio she'd made out of Addie's guest room, the windows open on this warm and sunny June morning. She had been working on a still life that consisted of a lapis-lazuli blue pottery jug, a crystal vase full of yellow roses out of Addie's garden and three Red Delicious apples on a white china plate. She had chosen those particular items for their difference in shapes, colors and textures, and had arranged them on a small table in front of the open window.

Absorbed in her work, it had taken her a while to realize that a fourth item had added itself to the arrangement. A four-legged item—now reared up on two—with its front paws draped along the rim of the pottery jug and its head all but buried inside it.

The cat!

It was hard to say who was the more startled, Bonnie at seeing Sam about to wreak havoc with her still life, or Sam by Bonnie's shrill little shriek. Both moved at about the same time, Bonnie to leap to her feet, in the process upsetting her easel, and Sam to leap off the table, upending the pottery pitcher and the vase of flowers in his hasty retreat.

To Bonnie's increased dismay, however, he didn't flee out the window through which he'd entered, but instead sought refuge elsewhere inside her house.

With another garbled shriek, Bonnie gave chase and, after some pretty fancy dodging and zigzagging through the kitchen and living room, finally cornered the cat in her bedroom. Sam was perched, hissing and spitting, his tail whipping back and forth, on top of Grandma Addie's high, old-fashioned maple wardrobe. Slitted yellow eyes dared Bonnie to come any closer.

Her chest heaving as she tried to catch her breath both from the chase and from the fright she'd gotten at spotting the cat amidst her artful display, Bonnie met him glare for glare. She was trying to collect her scattered thoughts and come up with a way of getting that cat down from there and out of her part of the house. Voluntarily.

"All right, cat," she finally announced, "here's the plan. You get off of there and out of the house, and we'll forget the whole thing ever happened."

Sam's only reply was to wiggle his calico bulk into a menacing crouch, as if getting ready to launch himself at her, and all the while his tail continued to sweep the dust off the wardrobe and into Bonnie's face.

Intimidated, she stepped back a pace. She wasn't used to dealing with animals, at least not the four-legged kind. Then she recalled that assertiveness sometimes worked with the two-legged variety she'd come across, so she took a deep breath and squared her shoulders. Animals were animals, after all.

Keeping her eyes firmly fixed on the cat's mesmerizing yellow ones and taking care to keep her voice firm and level, she repeated, "I said, get off of there, cat. Get off *now* and go home."

Muted applause sounded from behind her. Bonnie felt her face go red. She knew without even turning around that Frank Malloy had come to the rescue, but she turned to look at him anyway.

He stood with one shoulder propped against the doorjamb of her bedroom and looked sexy as sin again in sweatpants and nothing else. "I heard a crash," he said, his eyes assessing her as rapidly as hers were assessing him. "Need any help?"

His amused drawl grated. Bonnie tossed her head. "Does it look like I do?"

"Frankly, yes."

"Well, then—" Just at that moment the cat's proximity and the dust his tail continued to raise caught up with Bonnie. She sneezed. Fast and furious, a whole string of lusty *hachoo*s. "*Do* something!" she wailed.

Frank pulled a tissue out of his pocket and handed it to her. "Anything else?"

Noisily blowing her nose, Bonnie merely glared at him.

Frank grinned. "Right," he said, and turned his attention to the cat. "Scat, Sam."

Sam looked at him, obviously not any more impressed by the tone of command in Frank's voice than Bonnie was. He yawned and then, with an air of supreme boredom, settled down to do some serious washing.

Frank turned to Bonnie with a shrug of apology. "Cats can be difficult," he explained. Looking at her, he got sidetracked into thinking that Bonanza looked quite adorable with her hair in pigtails. And that the short shorts she was wearing displayed her long, shapely legs to perfection. Not that there was a damn thing wrong with the way her tank top hugged her obviously braless bosom.

She had the prettiest damn eyes, too, Frank hastened to note, when—as now—she didn't hide them behind those owly specs of hers....

He blessed the cat for giving him an excuse to be in his landlady's part of the house, for providing him with the opportunity to get to know her better, and he silently promised Sam a catnip treat later on.

But Frank also surprised himself not a little when he caught himself wishing he could come into this bedroom again under different, more personally satisfying circumstances. Had he lied to Eleanor Grimes—and to himself? Was it not merely platonic interest in an old friend's family, but something less altruistic, more basic, that urged him toward Bonanza Coombs?

Perhaps not too untimely, another explosive series of sneezes reminded Frank of today's reason for being in Bonanza's bedroom. Setting his discomfiting musings aside, he turned brisk. "Mind if I stand on this chair?"

With her nose buried in a tissue, Bonnie mutely shook her head.

Frank pulled a ladderback chair up close to the wardrobe and stepped up on its seat. "All right now, Sam," he said, unceremoniously scooping the cat into his arms. "That's enough trouble for one day. Time to skedaddle."

Bonnie watched Frank walk out of the room with a sense of loss that bewildered and dismayed her. *Wait,* she found herself wanting to say. *Don't go yet.* What in the world was the matter with her?

She was lonely, that's what. She missed Ellie and her family, the hugs, the camaraderie, the sharing. She missed the kids she'd helped with at the day-care center. She hadn't yet started the art classes that three days ago she'd volunteered to teach at Saint Christopher's, and she sorely missed human contact and interaction.

She liked it here in Rivervale, but she was lonely. She longed for someone to talk to, someone to reach out to and ask for advice. If it weren't for Thursdays and Jack Trainer, Bonnie didn't know how she'd have coped this long with everything this new life of hers demanded.

Take the rent check Frank Malloy had brought her the other day, for instance. She'd had to get the teller at the bank to help her fill out the deposit slip so that she could put the money into the account Ellie had helped her open for her inherited twenty-five thousand. Banking wasn't something she'd had much occasion to do in her life, and so she found even the hushed coolness of the place intimidating. She could only hope Frank would remember to do as she'd asked and pay her in cash from now on.

Bonnie trailed him out into the hall, then stood at the bottom of the stairs and watched him climb them. Of course, she mused, there was no way she'd ever be able to confide in Frank Malloy all the things that troubled and bewildered her, but it sure would be nice if they could just, well, *talk* now and then. If they could maybe share a cup of coffee, or even—yuk—tea....

As if aware of her scrutiny, about halfway to his landing, Frank stopped. He turned to look back. His free hand was stroking the cat who stretched and settled more closely into his arms.

Bonnie watched the movement of Frank's hand, watched Sam's satisfied reaction, and an ache of longing closed her throat. Just once in her life she'd like to have someone stroke her and pet her and care for her. Really care for her the way she sensed Frank Malloy cared for that animal.

Her eyes lifted to Frank's. They were dark blue and intense. Their caring expression made Bonnie's breath catch, made her long to rush up to him and beg for his touch. Unable to look away, she wrapped her arms tightly around the newel post, as if afraid she really would run after him if she let go. She ventured a tentative smile.

"Thanks for coming down to help."

A crooked smile of response lightened Frank's rugged face. "Hey, he's my cat. It's the least I can do."

"I don't suppose you'd like some coffee?" Bonnie went on, encouraged by the smile and the fact that he hadn't walked on. "After you put the cat into your apartment and wash your hands, that is."

"Hey, I'd love to, but..." Frank regretfully glanced at his watch.

She'd put him on the spot. Instantly mortified, Bonnie wished she could take back her impulsive invitation.

"On second thought," she said hurriedly, and found herself speaking with him simultaneously.

He was saying, "You see, I have to be at work in an hour and I haven't showered yet."

"Oh."

"I'll take a rain check," he added with an endearingly hopeful inflection.

"Sure." Face saved, Bonnie beamed. "You're on. Come anytime."

Frank nodded, jauntily climbed up a couple more steps, then paused to look down at her once again. "You know," he said, "there's antihistamine pills you can take for allergies like yours."

"Antihi—" Bonnie's tongue tripped over the difficult word. *"What?"*

"Antihistamines," Frank repeated, enunciating more clearly. "Just ask the druggist at Milton's Pharmacy, he'll know."

Bonnie returned the little wave Frank sent her, but stayed where she was until he'd disappeared. Antihistamines.

As soon as his door closed, she raced back into her bedroom, grabbed her purse and, repeating the word to herself over and over, headed for the drugstore.

"Antihistamines are on the shelf over there," the druggist told her, pointing. "Aisle four, by the cold medicines."

"I see. Thank you." Bonnie looked in the direction he indicated, saw the big number four on the sign, and smiled her relief. "Thank you," she repeated.

At aisle four, however, she was confronted by three long shelves filled with a bewildering array of tubes, bottles and packages. She tentatively picked one up, studied it with consternation wrinkling her brow, then put it back and picked up another. After several discouraging moments, she became aware of being watched. As if caught stealing, she flushed hotly and set down the package.

Casting a furtive glance to the side, her eyes met the curious gaze of a woman maybe ten years older than herself.

"You're Bonnie Coombs, aren't you?" the woman said, her tone friendly.

"Why, yes, I am."

"I'm Marie Donelly," the woman said, introducing herself, then she paused expectantly, almost as if she thought the name would mean something to Bonnie.

It didn't. And, "Hi" was all Bonnie could think of to say in reply to the introduction. Lord, but she wished for Ellie's gift of the gab and easy way with people. Maybe here was her chance to make a new friend, if only she didn't blow it. "I—I'm looking for antihistamines," she awkwardly explained.

"Oh. Well, there's enough of 'em, that's for sure," Marie swept an encompassing glance across the shelf.

"Can't make up your mind which brand to get, is that it?"

"Well, no, it's not that." There went that troublesome blush again. Bonnie inwardly despaired when, as it always did in situations like this, an anxiety sweat popped out all over her body. "I—it's..." she stammered. "I..."

"What?" Marie prompted kindly.

So kindly that Bonnie blurted out, "I can't read." And she could have instantly swallowed her tongue when she saw the woman's expression of fascinated disbelief.

"Th-the labels, I mean," she quickly amended, nearly sick with mortification. She put a hand to her eyes in a gesture of distress, noted that she wasn't wearing her glasses and dropped her hand. "It's my glasses, you see," she explained, falling back on a well-worn ploy. "I—I left home in such a hurry, I forgot to bring them."

"Oh. Of course." Marie's expression cleared, though she kept looking at Bonnie with the same searching concern she'd exhibited from the start. "Well, I'd be glad to help you find what you want. What's it for?"

"Allergies."

"Yes, of course. But what kind exactly? What're you allergic to?"

"Oh. Umm." Still thoroughly rattled by all that had transpired, Bonnie swallowed tears which were pooling, unbidden and unwelcome, at the back of her throat. Her need to cry made her furious, but mostly she was upset because she had vowed never to let herself get into predicaments like this ever again.

She had done so well until now, too. Ellie had made arrangements for all the eventualities they'd been able to think of. She'd shown Bonnie which bus to take to Olympia and back, and she'd gone with Bonnie to the bank and squared things there. Together they had scouted out all the stores Bonnie would need, including the one that carried art supplies. She'd been all set.

Until Frank Malloy came along, spouting off about *antihistamines*.

In just a few more months, she'd have been able to make out a fancy word like that, no sweat. But in the meantime, what on earth had possessed her to come into this store and make a fool of herself in public? In front of this woman?

"I'm allergic to cats," she finally told Marie Donelly with all the dignity she could muster. "Frank Malloy—he's my tenant—"

"I know," Marie interrupted with a grin. "Frank's my brother. That's how I knew you."

"Your...? Really?" Bonnie gaped, surprise overcoming the discomfiture of moments ago. This nice woman was Frank's sister. She looked at Marie more closely and found Frank's navy blue eyes twinkling back at her. Other than that, however, the physical resemblance was only slight. Where Frank was ruddy and dark, Marie was pink and fair....

"Really," Marie laughingly insisted. "I can't believe he hasn't mentioned Jennifer and me to you."

"Jennifer?"

"My daughter. The niece Frank claims to dote on." She shook her head in exasperation. "To think he hasn't told you."

Bonnie relaxed, thinking, she could really like this woman. "To be honest," she said, "he and I don't talk all that much. Matter of fact, I hardly see him, he works such crazy hours."

"Tell me about it." Marie rolled her vivid eyes. "I work the same hours, as often as not."

"You do? How come?"

"You mean he hasn't told you that, either?" Looking disgusted, Marie flashed a badge. "We're cops, Frank and I. Like all the Malloys."

Chapter Four

A cop. She had a lousy, stinking *P-I-G,* cop, living under her roof.

Bonnie yanked off her glasses, tossed them aside and massaged her temples. The sun was shining with a vengeance, her guest bedroom-cum-studio was lit to perfection, and yet she couldn't paint to save her life because the "Greek god" who made her temperature rise and her ceilings creak had turned out to be a *policeman.*

Even in her thoughts she spat the word.

Policemen had hounded her most of her life it seemed. Not always alone, sometimes child-welfare workers had been by their side. But always they had spelled trouble. Or, at least, change. Which invariably led to trouble, so there you were.

Foster homes—Bonnie had forgotten how many. Too many, that was for sure. And none of them had

had for her what she so desperately craved: love, the unconditional kind. The kind that understood she was able to draw better than she liked to write or figure. The kind that knew she wasn't really bad, only lost. The kind that knew all she ever wanted was a mother and a father of her own.

But her mother hadn't wanted her and her father never came for her, and so Bonnie had done a lot of running. Not so much *away from* as *toward,* and though she'd been the only one to know the difference, she would have had trouble explaining it. She never found what she was looking for, either, though she usually did find trouble. Or trouble found her—as often as not in the form of a policeman who'd none-too-gently yank her off the streets and toss her into custody until some busybodying agency or other dug up another foster home. After which the cycle would repeat itself all over again.

Until Whitworth. And Ellie. And now this house here in Rivervale. Bonnie had begun to feel safe here, and at home. So much so that she'd begun to relax around Frank Malloy, the attractive man upstairs whose presence had, in the beginning, scared the living daylights out of her. She'd allowed herself to be drawn to him, and she'd just begun to be okay with that.

No one but Ellie knew that, given Bonnie's history, those things were no mean accomplishments.

Bonnie's earliest memories were of men, lots of men. Of men coming and going in their house. Of men making her mother—making *Loretta*—moan and shrilly laugh or sometimes scream. And she remembered some of those men reaching for her, too, touching and frightening the child Bonnie had been. All except one man.

Roy Rogers Filmore.

He'd told Bonnie he was her father, and she'd been ecstatic to know she did have one, after all. He never hurt her, either; he was nice. He didn't come to see Bonnie very often, not nearly as often as she'd have liked him to, and he didn't take her away the way he'd promised he would and she'd wished so very hard. But he did bring presents, and he gave gentle hugs.

Best of all, though, whenever he was there, her mother would be sober. She'd treat Bonnie nice, and let her wear nice clothes.

And then he didn't come anymore. . . .

Agitated, Bonnie jumped up from her chair and paced, both hands buried in her hair, clutching it as if to tear it out by the roots, arms pressed to her ears to shut out all sound. She had stood just so while Loretta rained blows on her head and shoulders, shrieking obscenities and accusations after the seven-year-old Bonnie had asked why her father never came anymore.

"Because he doesn't want you, that's why," Loretta had hollered. "You're rotten and stupid and nothin' but trouble. Who'd want an ugly brat like you? I sure's hell don't. . . ."

And then one day the cops had come, with fat old Sheriff Claymore in the lead. Only a week or so before, he'd snuck from Loretta's bed into Bonnie's. He'd grabbed her hand and put it on his fat old *thing*, but she had dug in her nails and twisted it, hard. He'd been furious, calling her names and slapping her in the mouth. But he'd left her alone after that until the day he showed up on their doorstep to take her away.

Loretta had stood on the porch in her old chenille robe, a pitiful drunk with spit spraying out through the gaps in her teeth and tears making streaks in the thick layers of makeup on her face.

"It's your own fault," she'd yelled after Bonnie, clutching the doorjamb and weaving on her feet. "Yours and that no-good daddy o' yours, so don't go blamin' me for nothin', you hear me?"

Bonnie had heard, all right, while she'd been busy biting and screaming, though none of it had done her any good. Sheriff Claymore had twisted her arm until she thought it'd pop clear out of its socket, and he'd dragged her along and slammed her into his patrol car.

"You need to have yourself taught some manners, you little slut," he'd said in that whiskey-hoarse, scratchy voice of his, and on the way to the county home he'd pulled the car off onto a wooded side road and done just that.

Loretta had died when Bonnie was ten. Some guy she'd slept with had worked her over, splitting her skull. The day she was told was the day Bonnie had run away from the foster home they'd stuck her in.

It'd been the first of many such runs, none of which had ever taken her anywhere but into more trouble....

Slowly, stiffly, Bonnie lowered her arms and lifted her head. With eyes burning from unshed tears, she stared out of the window at the bright afternoon, the shade-dappled yard. But she saw neither. What she did see was herself as the object of contempt and ridicule in the schools they'd made her attend, but in which she'd refused to learn.

Was it time to run once again? she wondered dismally. Should she run before the policeman upstairs found out about her and spread it around? Run before everybody in town knew how bad a kid she'd been and the kind of mother she'd had? Before anyone got the chance to point at her and whisper the names the kids in school used to call her, as they crossed the street when they saw her coming?

Jerking away from the window, desperate for escape from her thoughts, Bonnie ran from the room, through the hall and kitchen and out the back door. She was halfway up the cracked cement walk by the side of her house, on her way to the tired old gate leading out to the street, when reason returned and with it, anger. Her steps first slowed, then stopped.

What the *hell* did she think she was doing? Running again? No, by God, she wouldn't. Not this time. Not anymore. She was done with that.

Suddenly exhausted, Bonnie let her head drop onto her chest. Eyes closed, she released a tremulous breath and, in need of support, propped a somewhat shaky hand against the wall of the house.

Her house. Her *home*. And she wouldn't run from it.

Beneath her palm, the siding felt warm. Bonnie let the warmth seep into her bones and drew comfort from it. Impulsively, she let the length of her body relax against it. Eyes still closed, she pressed her cheek to the wall. The slightly abrasive, blistered and peeling coat of paint felt good in much the same way her daddy's beard-roughened face had felt good touching hers.

Her daddy... With a choked half laugh, half cry, Bonnie turned her head and pressed her forehead against the wall. She hadn't thought of Roy Rogers Filmore in those terms since she couldn't remember when. She'd been too angry with him for not keeping his promise and for staying away.

Nor had she wondered, as she wondered now, if he truly had loved her the way he'd always said, and if— supposing he hadn't been killed—he might not have come for her after all.

She hadn't known he'd been killed until the lawyer had told her at the reading of Addie's will.

For the first time, with her body hugging the house in which her father had grown up, and with her nostrils full of the dusty smell of ancient paint mingling with the sweetness of peonies in bloom, she wondered how her life might have been different if she had known. Would she have been more content to be raised by strangers? Would she have been able to trust more? To accept the affection some of them had offered, the affection she'd viewed with suspicion and rejected out of hand, time and again? Instead of running away whenever a foster home began to feel too much like a real home, would she have been able to settle with one of the families—like the Juricks, for instance, they'd wanted a daughter so badly—and been adopted, the way other kids in her shoes often had been?

Maybe.

Turning so that her back was against the wall, Bonnie tilted her face up to the sun and let the realization that she hadn't been as completely unwanted and rejected as she'd thought fill her with additional warmth. It was too late to matter; knowing it didn't change anything. And yet . . .

"Hey, you asleep standin' up over there?"

Torn from her thoughts by the good-natured masculine voice, Bonnie gave a violent start. After blinking to focus, she saw in front of her a toothily grinning countenance and curling blond hair that stuck out from beneath a grease-stained ball cap.

From years of subterfuge and necessity, Bonnie's memory skills had been honed to perfection. Anything she heard or saw—be it a story, a poem, a picture or a face—that in some way impressed her, got indelibly stuck in her mind. She could then recall it whenever it became expedient to do so.

Now she knew, instantly, the name of the gangly young man with his arms folded atop the Savages' fence.

"Jimmy, wasn't it?" she said, keeping her tone as neutral as the facial expression she'd perfected for situations such as this. Wait And See, was her motto. Give away nothing until you knew which way the wind was blowing. "From the service station?"

He was the guy who'd been friendly to her and Ellie, who'd given them directions to this house.

"Hey, yeah." His grin spread; more teeth appeared. "I remember your name, too, because it's so weird."

Bonnie stiffened.

"You know, in a neat kind of way. *Bonanza*." He pronounced the word with such obvious relish, Bonnie couldn't help but warm toward him. "It has a ring to it, you know?"

"Yeah," she said, drily. "I know."

They looked at each other, Jimmy's grin not diminishing in wattage until Bonnie couldn't help but smile back.

This seemed to delight him. "Hey, Bonanza, you oughta smile more often. You know?"

Bonnie instantly sobered. What was she doing, trading silly looks and banter with this Jimmy character? What did he want from her, anyway? And what was he doing at the Savages'?

She pushed away from the wall, frowning. "Yeah, well, I've got to get busy."

"Gonna cut your grass?" Jimmy called after her as she walked away.

"What?" *Cut the grass?* There'd been no lawn in L.A. at Ellie's, just dirt and rocks that Ellie laughingly called "desert landscaping." Bonnie looked at the patch of green behind her house. The grass was lush and long, the way it hardly ever got in Southern California. She thought it looked great. "Why would I cut the grass? It looks great."

"You cut it 'cause you're supposed to. Everybody does."

"Not anybody *I* know."

"Who do you know?"

"Lots of people." More like two or three, really. "In California."

"Oh." It was obvious Californians didn't rank high on Jimmy's list. "Well, here people cut their grass. See—" He pointed behind himself to a mower. "I cut the grass over here. If you want to, I'll come do yours next.''

"No, thanks." In spite of herself, Bonnie was drawn into conversation with him. She kind of enjoyed it. He was easy to talk to. "I thought you worked at the gas station?''

"Part-time, yeah. Other times I do yard work for people and stuff like that. Like, I paint houses, too." He cast hers a pitying glance. "I wouldn't charge you much for painting yours. Or for doing some weeding, either."

"Really." Resentment at his implied criticism of her home had Bonnie's hackles rising. She gave him a look that had never failed to send her day-care charges into retreat. "Are you saying my place is a mess?''

Jimmy seemed unimpressed by her attitude. His grin never wavered and his shrug was eminently uncaring. "Nothin' some elbow grease and a little paint wouldn't fix."

"Oh, yeah?" But even as Bonnie laced the words with contempt, she mentally removed the rose-colored glasses through which she'd thus far viewed her inheritance and took a good look around. Jimmy was right, the once-white paint on the house was drab and flaky. In the flower beds, weeds were choking the life out of the rightful inhabitants, while most of the shrubbery branched beyond some of the windows in which, Bonnie was chagrined to note, the sun's rays were dully reflected. The place needed work, there were no two ways about it.

Once she'd admitted it to herself, resentment fled. In its place a glorious burst of energy materialized. Yes, she thought. Yes. Giving the house an overhaul was exactly what she needed to really make the place her own.

She turned back to Jimmy with a smile. "I guess I see what you mean," she said, and almost laughed aloud when his eyes popped open and he comically banged the heel of his hand against the side of his head at her unexpected about-face.

She shrugged. "What can I say, except that I guess I never *really* looked at the place before." She elaborated. "This is the first house I've ever owned." Something about Jimmy made him easy to open up with. "It's my first real home."

"Yeah?" Jimmy settled his chin on top of his arms, which still rested on the fence, and he gave the house another once-over. "Old Addie was your grandma, you say?"

"I didn't say." Wariness had become so much a part of her nature that Bonnie backed off without conscious intention.

"Your friend in the car, then. She said it."

"So if you know already, why're you asking?"

Jimmy's head came up. "Boy, you're touchy." His good-natured expression clouded. Bonnie felt mean and nasty, but told herself he was way too pushy, especially when he added, "I just wondered how come you didn't have a home before, that's all."

"That's none of your business, Jimmy...uh..."

Not being able to add his last name robbed the rebuke of its intended sharpness. "Say what's your last name, anyway?"

"Thurston. After the county."

"Well, Jimmy Thurston—" Bonnie had started anew when what he'd said hit home. "What do you mean, 'after the county'?"

He shrugged. "Thurston County, get it?"

When she continued to look blank, he sighed disgustedly. "You know, the one we're in right now? Someone found me on a doorstep or somethin'."

When Bonnie only kept staring, he obviously took her silence for contempt. "Hey, we can't all have doting grandmas, you know. Jeez . . ."

He swung away, angry. Or was he hurt?

Either way, Bonnie found she couldn't just let him go. She ran up to the fence. "I never knew I had one, either," she called. And when he looked at her again, she told him what she'd never voluntarily told anyone else before. "I mostly grew up in foster homes and such."

Now it was Jimmy's turn to stare, and in the course of the ensuing long and silent eye contact, a bond of sorts was forged between them. Slowly, sheepish smiles blossomed, and then they both laughed, a bit self-consciously. After a while, Jimmy, still chortling and shaking his head, tossed her a half salute and, with a mighty yank on the cord, started his mower.

Bonnie, feeling better inside than she ever had, watched him for a while, inhaling and savoring the smell of freshly cut grass Jimmy left in his wake. And then she headed toward the shed in back of her own yard, in search of a lawn mower.

When Frank got home and looked out of his back window, the sight he beheld confounded him. Why, he wondered, would Bonanza Coombs be on her hands and knees in the grass digging up dandelion plants and then, instead of tossing them into the yard-waste bin the town provided, carry them carefully over to Addie's new fallow vegetable patch to plant them there?

He stepped out onto his small porch just in time to hear that very question put into words by the Thurston kid, who was hanging over the fence. Frank surmised from the tone that this wasn't the first conversational exchange between his inimitable landlady and Jimmy Thurston.

"*Now* what're you doin'?" Jimmy asked with visible consternation. "Those're weeds."

"Says who?" Bonnie tenderly mounded soil around her latest transplant.

"Says *everybody*." Jimmy was looking disgusted as he repeated. "Dandelion's a *weed*, Bonanza, and I'm telling ya, you don't want 'em in your yard."

"Well, how do you know that?" Agitated, Bonnie shot to her feet. She planted soiled fists on both hips and glared fiercely at the astonished Jimmy Thurston.

Up on his deck, unnoticed by the two below, Frank leaned forward to better hear what Bonnie had to say.

"After what you told me a while ago, you're the last person I'd have expected to hear say something stupid like that." She stalked closer to the fence but—fortunately for Frank—didn't lower her voice. "What gives you or anybody the right to decide what's a good plant and what's a bad one and where each of them can grow, huh? Who gets to decide what's a flower and what's a weed?"

"Jeez, Bonanza . . ."

"I'll tell you who, Jimmy Thurston—the same kind of people who decided that we—that's you and me, bud—that we weren't as good as they were, that's who. And you're buying that crap."

Intrigued, disturbed, Frank watched and listened while half of his mind wondered how and when Bonnie and Jimmy had met and become friends. He knew Jim—and his history—from Saint Christopher's where, over the years, Jimmy had been at times resident, at times drop-in visitor, and where he now did most of the odd jobs in addition to giving Frank a good workout in a game of one-on-one basketball every week.

The Jimmy he knew wasn't one to be caught at a loss for words as a rule, but Bonnie's harangue definitely seemed to have rendered him speechless. He was gaping at her as at an alien from Mars, with eyes rounded and jaw slack, and was no doubt asking himself how in the world they'd gotten from dandelions to the human condition.

"Are you saying people can't live wherever they want?" Bonnie demanded, practically nose to nose with Jimmy now. "Are you saying I don't belong here in this town, for instance? Or in this house? Are you, huh?"

Jimmy drew back, blinking. "Well, jeez, no, Bonanza," he protested. "That's not what I'm sayin' at all...."

"Then what *are* you saying, Jimmy Thurston?"

Jimmy screwed up his face, whipped off his cap and mopped his brow. "I'm sayin' dandelions're weeds, that's all." He slapped the cap back into place and with a black look at Bonnie, spun on his heel and stalked to his mower. "And I'm still sayin' it."

"And I think they're not. So there." Bonnie, too, pivoted sharply, glancing up at Frank's porch as she did.

As their gazes connected, Frank raised a hand in greeting and smiled, only to have the smile wither and fade when Bonnie's expression of grim triumph turned merely grim, then grimmer still.

Without either acknowledging or returning his greeting, she abruptly turned around and bent over Addie's dilapidated old lawn mower. Viciously, she yanked the cord, which promptly succumbed to age and exposure and broke.

Momentum planted Bonnie neatly onto her backside.

Frank might have laughed at the spectacle had he not been so puzzled and perturbed by the snub he'd just received. Hadn't they parted amicably as recently as yesterday? He frowned. Hadn't there been talk of coffee, and rain checks, and hadn't she actually smiled at him? Sure, all of that. So how come she was back to giving him the cold shoulder just twenty-four hours later?

He was down the outside stairs in moments and asking Bonnie that very thing.

"What's wrong?" She was kneeling next to the mower, trying—unsuccessfully—to knot together the torn starter cord. She neither looked up nor acknowledged his question.

"Dammit, Bonanza—" abruptly out of patience, Frank reached across her shoulder, took the string from her hand and tossed it aside "—I'm talking to you." Gripping her under each armpit, he unceremoniously hauled her to her feet.

Furious, Bonnie jerked free and whirled to face him. "But I'm *not* talking to you, Officer Malloy, so go away."

Frank's eyebrows rose, not so much in response to her puzzling change in attitude as to the scornful contempt with which she laced the word *officer.* She made it sound as if in her book it wasn't a title so much as an epithet. Eleanor Grimes had warned him, hadn't she?

Scowling, Frank watched Bonnie tromp over to the garden hose and fill the watering can. And he wondered yet again what it was had made her view his profession with such obvious contempt. It was clear she'd only just found out what he did for a living. From whom? And could it really be he hadn't mentioned it himself?

Even as he asked himself, he knew he hadn't. Hell, until yesterday they really hadn't had a heck of a lot to say to each other, period, let alone exchange personal histories and such. Not after the rocky start they'd had. So who *had* told her, and what had been said to make her so mad at him all over again?

Bonanza has a thing about cops. Ellie Grimes had made that quite clear in the course of their telephone conversation. What she hadn't said was what that "thing" was.

Determined to find out, Frank marched over to where Bonnie was now watering the transplanted dandelions. There were seven plants in all, richly in bloom and, Frank had to admit, though he'd never stopped to think about it before, they were actually very pretty.

"I liked that weed-versus-flower business you said to Jimmy earlier," he said, opting for diplomacy rather than the foot-first approach he seemed to be prone to around this woman.

"Buzz off, Malloy."

"Not until you tell me what the hell's eating you." To hell with diplomacy. "I was under the impression we'd arrived at a truce yesterday."

"If we did, it's over now." Bonnie went back for more water, though the dandelions were practically floating as it was.

Frank was right behind her. "I'd like to know why."

She spared him a frigid glance before heading back to the vegetable patch. "You're a cop," she said. "I don't like cops. I don't talk to cops. I don't want a cop anywhere in my life."

Which wasn't quite true, Bonnie thought with a sharp sense of regret. She'd very much like Malloy's sister, Marie Donelly, for a friend, in spite of her profession, though she doubted Marie felt the same. She'd probably resent Bonnie's aversion to her brother.

"Care to tell me why?" that brother demanded.

"No."

"Do you think that's fair?"

That got to her. Bonnie slammed the watering can down. Water sloshed all over her sneakers, soaking them. She whirled to face him.

"Fair?" she exclaimed with red-faced fury. "Fair? Is it fair to drag a little kid away from her home, rotten though it may be, when she doesn't want to go? Is it? Huh? Is it fair to sexually abuse a kid and call it 'teaching manners'? Is that fair?''

Bonnie was working herself into a fine rage as accumulated grievances and injustices clamored to be aired. All of the worrying she'd done since yesterday popped like puss from a wound that had festered way too long. ''Is it fair to lock kids up just because they've got no place to go? To treat them like dirt, like *things* with no feelings, no rights? Is that fair, *Officer* Malloy?''

''Detective,'' Frank corrected absently, his mind on her charges. He was appalled by the pictures they conjured up in his mind, horrified by the knowledge that she spoke from personal experience, and he was heartsick because there was nothing he could say to change the past.

''There's good and bad in every profession, Bonanza,'' he finally told her, knowing the words were inadequate.

''Yeah.'' She snorted in disgust. ''That's what they say. Cops, that is. Those on the receiving end say something else, believe me.''

''I do believe you,'' Frank said. ''But I wish you'd believe me when I tell you I've never hurt anybody.''

''Haven't you? Well . . .'' She started to brush past him, but when she was abreast of him, she stopped and looked him coldly in the eye. ''Give it time. You will.''

Chapter Five

Bonnie strode away, shoulders set and head high, before Frank could collect himself sufficiently to make a response. He watched her departure with furrowed brows and a powerful mixture of emotions that vacillated between irritation and sympathy, with in between, a whole mess of feelings he'd really prefer not to examine too closely.

His irritation stemmed from resentment. Resentment about the fact that Bonanza Coombs, after having him under her roof for more than a month and after they'd arrived at an understanding of sorts with each other that morning, could out of the blue turn on him the way she had. He didn't deserve it. And he damn well didn't like it.

Still, he felt sympathy for her, too, and pain. Pain that was very similar to, but stronger than, the pain he experienced whenever evidence of human suffering

confronted him. Call him a softie—many of his colleagues did, while others called him worse—but the
fact was, he believed that people, and especially the
young, ran afoul of the law for a reason. And more
often than not, in his experience and opinion, that
reason was rooted in the hurts they received during the
daily lives of their childhoods.

Having had nothing but the best in his own forma-
tive years—an extensive and loving family, a quiet
community, a good home and good schools, along
with regular meals and plenty of opportunities—it
pained him to know that all too many youngsters had
few or none of those things.

It killed him to think Bonanza had been one of
those youngsters.

Which brought him to the feelings he'd as soon not
try to define. Suffice to say they culminated in an urge
to do physical violence to every single person who had
ever caused Bonanza Coombs unhappiness. Those
members of his honorable profession who'd misused
the power with which they'd been entrusted were first
in line.

As he watched Bonanza hurry away from him, the
rigid posture of her retreating form struck him as a
sign of such utter vulnerability, of a loneliness so profound, he felt emotion ballooning in his throat, closing it. He wanted to rush after her, to scoop her up and
hold her close and keep her safe. Forever.

The urge was so powerful, the thought so alien and
scary, sweat popped out all over Frank's body. He
forced himself to look away, blindly cast around for
something—anything—else to focus on. Which was
when he saw the lawn mower, with its torn bit of

starter cord and its rusting, once-red body. As if it were to blame for everything that had transpired, Frank kicked it. Worthless piece of junk, he thought viciously. Addie should have trashed the thing years ago.

Next, Frank glared at the lawn, overgrown and shaggy, the mounds of dirt from Bonnie's digging dotting it like blackheads on a bum's face. How come he hadn't noticed till now what a mess it had become? Addie must be spinning in her grave. He was going to cut the thing, by damn.

With grim purpose, he strode up to the fence. "Hey, Thurston," he hollered to Jimmy, who was now busily pulling weeds, "I need to borrow that mower of yours."

"Help yourself." Jimmy went on with his work while Frank walked to the small gate at the end of the yard. Moments later, he had the mower's engine roaring and was marching smartly up and down the lawn.

With arms hugging her middle, her feelings a riot of contradiction, Bonnie stood at the kitchen window and watched Frank Malloy cut her grass. The white sheers through which she was looking cloaked the scene outside in a foggy haze, softening and blurring it and giving it a dreamlike, unreal quality that further muddied her emotional waters.

What, she asked herself, was real and what was not? Who was Frank Malloy, really? A ruthless cop like so many she'd encountered, or the decent and caring man he'd consistently presented himself to be? He had never given her a reason to doubt he was anything but the latter, so why was it she seemed to prefer to cast him in the role of villain?

She'd done it right from the start, she admitted with characteristic but—just then—not entirely welcome honesty. She had taken one look at the darkly handsome man on her doorstep and, with reaction making her heart turn cartwheels in her chest, had decided right then and there that, a) she didn't like him, b) she didn't trust him—men that handsome were always too full of themselves and too sure of their power over the opposite sex—and c) she wanted him nowhere near her.

Yet, hadn't she come to realize in the weeks since then that she had grown to like him quite a bit? And hadn't she taken comfort from the knowledge that, should the need arise, he'd come to her aid if she called?

Sure, she'd fought those feelings, and she'd looked for reasons to be annoyed with him—the footsteps overhead, the cat, the music—but that had been a defense mechanism born from force of habit. She was slow to make friends and even slower to trust. Too often in the past she'd had friendly overtures rejected and her trust betrayed, but with Malloy she'd begun to relax.

Only to find out he was a cop.

A *policeman,* she mentally corrected, though not consciously aware of doing so, or of the more respectful intonation she was giving the word in her mind. There was no way in the world she could ever like or trust a policeman.

Was there?

Watching Malloy stride back and forth across her lawn, grim purpose in his step and in the expression on his face, the collar of his pin-striped dress shirt unbuttoned and his tie loosened—

His *tie?* Blinking, Bonnie choked on sudden laughter. Good Lord—Frank Malloy was out there in a shirt, tie and tan dress slacks, cutting her grass. He'd shed the tweedy sport coat he'd worn when he'd come down from the porch to talk to her. It hung on a branch of the old pear tree.

Something twisted in her stomach, something Bonnie was tempted to call nausea, but she was aware that wasn't it at all. It was something much more profound, much more frightening. It was something like what she'd used to feel as a little kid whenever Roy Rogers Filmore—whenever her *dad*—would show up at their doorstep, unexpected, and bring her something wonderful like a new baby doll or candy or some such surprise. She'd get all tingly and warm inside then, and she'd hug him so hard....

A stinging sensation in her eyes was blurring the shape of the man outside and Bonnie abruptly turned her back to the window. Impatience with herself had her harshly applying knuckles to eyeballs, dashing away any unwelcome moisture there. So Malloy had his good sides, just as Roy Filmore'd had, too. So what did that prove? Had old Roy stuck around, been there when she'd needed him?

A choked sort of snort escaped her. Hell, no. As to cops having their good sides, sure they did. Hadn't she been in the same grade as one of Sheriff Claymore's granddaughters, and didn't little Nancy Wambaugh all the time tell everybody about her dynamite grandpa? There were good sides to everybody.

Trouble was— Head bent, brow furrowed, Bonnie walked over to the table and stared down at the sketchbook she'd been doodling in earlier that day. Trouble was, when it came to Bonanza Coombs, sooner or later people's bad sides took over.

Maybe if she'd been prettier or smarter. Maybe if she'd stuck it out somewhere instead of always running, or if she'd tried harder to make sense of those confounded squiggles teachers called the alphabet, the way she did now. Maybe then things might have been different, people might have been nicer....

Slowly, immersed in her thoughts, Bonnie traced the features of the face on the page of her sketchbook with her finger. It was a strong face, a handsome face. It was the face of...Frank Malloy.

Bonnie snatched back her finger, flipped the page. Malloy again. And again on the next page. *Damn*—

The doorbell rang.

With a violent start, feeling as if she'd been caught doing something illicit, Bonnie slammed her sketchbook shut and, for lack of a better, handier place, shoved it beneath the seat cushion of the captain's chair at the head of the kitchen table.

With the bell chiming impatiently yet again, she ran to get the door. Opening it, she was confronted by a toothily grinning, raven-haired moppet whose smile dropped from her face the instant she caught sight of Bonnie.

"Yo-you're n-not," the child stuttered, with something like fear expanding already huge sapphire blue eyes to saucers as she backed away from the door. "You're not A-Ad-die."

"No, I'm not." Dumbfounded, Bonnie cast a quick look beyond the child, saw no one and hunkered down. They solemnly regarded each other for a while, and then slowly, tentatively, the little girl's smile returned.

"W-who're you?" she asked.

"I'm Bonanza," Bonnie told her with an answering smile. For all the reserve she exhibited in the presence of adults, when dealing with children, she was invariably comfortable, relaxed and outgoing. "But my friends call me Bonnie."

"Is—is Uncle F-Frankie your f-friend?" the child asked, confirming Bonnie's growing suspicion—how many eyes of such striking color could there be, after all?—that this was a member of the Malloy family.

"Well . . ." She was still casting around for a reply that wasn't a lie, when Marie Donelly rounded the corner of the house. She'd obviously gone to greet her brother in the backyard and was now in search of her daughter.

"Jennifer Donelly!" she scolded fondly. "I've been looking for you." She came up on the porch and took the little girl's hand. "Why didn't you come to say hi to Uncle Frank?"

"I w-w-wanted t-t-to v-visit w-with A-Ad-die. . . ." The child's stutter became noticeably pronounced in the face of her mother's disapproval.

Bonnie, too, felt discomfited by Marie Donelly's presence, if for reasons other than those that troubled Jennifer. She remembered the humiliating way she and the other woman had parted that afternoon in Milton's Pharmacy.

Shocked by what she'd just learned about Marie and her brother—namely that they were both on the police force—Bonnie had mumbled something inane and unintelligible, grabbed the nearest package of antihistamines and bolted from the store. Without paying.

Both Marie and the drugstore cashier had come running out onto the sidewalk after Bonnie and, just as in the nightmares that still sometimes haunted her, an all too familiar scenario out of the past had ensued.

With the cashier shouting something like, "Stop, thief," and half the town gawking, someone had grabbed hold of Bonnie's arm and held her until Marie and the other woman could catch up. Whereupon the cashier had yanked the small package out of Bonnie's lifeless fingers and proceeded to give her a tongue lashing that Marie had tried unsuccessfully to interrupt by repeating a soothing, "Now, Mabel."

It wasn't until everyone there had gotten quite an earful and Bonnie wanted nothing so much as for the ground to open up and swallow her that Marie's sternly threatening "Mabel Wilkins, that's enough!" had put an end to the spectacle. Saying, "Go about your business, folks, there's been a mistake. This woman is a friend of mine," Marie had briskly dispersed the crowd and firmly put the package back into Bonnie's hand.

"I'm sorry," she'd said to Bonnie before addressing the still red-faced drugstore clerk. "Look here, Mabel, Ms. Coombs got distracted by something I said and simply forgot about the purchase she'd meant to

make. I'm sure you know how that goes sometimes...."

After some hesitation, Mabel had allowed that, yes,
she knew how that could happen, but she'd balked a
bit more when Marie suggested, "I think we both owe
her an apology, don't you?"

At which point Bonnie had roused herself sufficiently to utter a feeble, "Oh, no, please," before
she'd once again gotten the heck out of there. With the
pills, and with her reputation in shreds, but without
dignity.

And, she suddenly remembered with an icy splash
of shock, still without paying!

Oh, no! What must Marie Donelly be thinking? No
wonder she was scolding her child for being here with
Bonnie on the porch instead of in the back with her
mother and uncle.

Bonnie quickly straightened from her crouch in
front of Jennifer. She'd go get the money right now—
Marie had probably paid it—and spare them all further embarrassment.

Inching backward across the doorstep into the
house, Bonnie heard Marie say to Jennifer, "Honey,
Addie doesn't live here anymore. Remember how
Uncle Frank told you a while ago that she passed away
and—"

"L-like m-my d-daddy?" Anguish quivered in the
child's voice, and Bonnie felt her own chest constrict.
She well knew the pain of losing a daddy.

"Yes, love," Marie said gently. "Like that."

"Oh." A world of sadness in such a little word.

Sharing that sadness, Bonnie fumbled in the purse

she kept hanging on the coatrack in the hall and pulled out a five-dollar bill. As she hurried back out on the porch with it, Jennifer was saying, "B-but, Mama, you, you s-said we were g-going to Uncle F-Frank's house t-to see a f-friend . . ."

"And so we are." Marie lifted warmly smiling eyes to Bonnie's. "We came to see Bonnie. She's our friend, aren't you, Bonnie?"

"Yes," Jennifer piped up excitedly before Bonnie could dislodge a sudden lump in her throat. "Yes, sh-she is, Mama, 'cause—'cause she t-told me all her f-friends c-call her B-Bonnie, and—and you c-called her Bonnie, Mama."

She gave Bonnie a smile so sweet, Bonnie almost dropped to her knees again to give the child a big hug. Almost. The sight of Frank Malloy scowling as he pushed the lawn mower onto the tiny patch of lawn in the front yard stopped her. His sister had probably told him all about the fiasco at the drugstore and she'd just sunk another few notches in his esteem.

With crimson heat scorching her cheeks, she held the money out to Marie. "Here," she said, "I hope it's enough."

"What?" Clearly startled, Marie stared at the bill. "Enough for what?"

"The pills. The antihistamines," Bonnie elaborated, for once taking no pleasure in the easy way this difficult word rolled from her tongue. "Remember? From that afternoon at the drugstore . . . ?"

"Oh, that." Marie pulled a face. "Forget it."

"No, please, I'm sorry. I should've paid you sooner; you shouldn't have had to come by for it.

I—'' She caught Marie's hand and tried to place the five dollars into it.

"Is that what you think?" Marie yanked her hand out of Bonnie's light hold. "That I came for the money?"

"Well . . ."

"Oh, for crying out loud." With an exasperated little laugh, Marie took Bonnie's elbow and steered her into the house. "Go say hello to Uncle Frank, Squirt," she said to Jennifer. "Mom wants to talk with Bonnie for a bit."

"All right." Jennifer went to obey, but cast a doleful glance back at Bonnie. "S-see you."

"You bet. Come in and have some lemonade, okay?" To Marie, Bonnie said, "What a darling little girl."

"Yeah." Marie's gaze, following her daughter's sedate progress down the front steps, was clouded. "Time was she bounced everywhere she went and talked our ears off."

"What happened?"

"Her father died."

"Oh." Bonnie didn't know what to say or how to express the empathy she felt.

"All the life went out of her," Marie went on, "the day we laid him in the ground. And she's stuttered ever since."

"Poor kid." Moved by Marie's words and troubled by them, too, Bonnie glanced once more at Jennifer. She stood on the bottom step of the porch, her eyes still on Bonnie.

"What is it, honey?" Bonnie called.

"Can, can Uncle F-Frank c-come have some lemonade, t-too?"

Startled by the request, Bonnie's gaze flew to Frank, and wouldn't you know he'd choose that very moment to look her way. Without a scowl this time, but with an expression which, for all it only lasted the length of a heartbeat, forcefully brought home to Bonnie the fact that her jean cutoffs were very short and her cotton tanktop had shrunk a size in the dryer. Thanks to her unsettled emotional state, as well as the day's humidity, it clung damply to her body, and Malloy was looking at her the way Sylvester the cat eyed Tweetie Pie the canary—with hunger, and longing.

"S-sure," Bonnie muttered distractedly in reply to Jennifer's question, bothered by Frank's intent perusal in a tinglingly delicious sort of way. Face aflame, she tore her eyes away from Frank's, only to encounter Marie Donelly's thoughtful gaze.

"At home," Marie remarked with a twinkle brightening her eyes, "growing up, Mom always had to threaten Frank with house arrest before he'd do the grass. What did you threaten him with?"

"Why, nothing." Bonnie hated the flush she felt heating her face again and tried to shrug off her self-consciousness with a breathy little laugh. "I looked out the window and there he was, doing it."

"And here they say chivalry is dead," Marie quipped, deadpan, and then, catching Bonnie's puzzled look, laughed. "Don't mind me. It's just so...*refreshing* to see my brother exercising his green thumb for a change. And in his office clothes yet. My, my..." She laughed again and caught Bonnie's arm.

"Come on, let's go inside before he mistakes our watching him for admiration and gets a swelled head."

A little uncertainly, Bonnie joined Marie's laughter.

"Have a seat," she said to Marie as they entered the kitchen.

"Thanks." Marie looked around approvingly. "Nothing's changed. I'm glad. I always liked Addie's kitchen."

"Did you come see her often?" Bonnie asked, pulling a frosted pitcher of lemonade from the refrigerator and some glasses from the cupboard. Marie, too, it seemed, had been a friend of her grandmother.

"Hmm. Thanks." Marie took the glass Bonnie held out to her, adding, "A couple of times a month, I'd say. Addie really liked Jennifer, and Jennifer really liked Sam—"

"The cat?"

"Addie's cat, yes."

"Addie's cat? I thought Sam belonged to Fr—to your brother."

"He does now. Addie made Frank promise to take care of him."

"Oh," Bonnie said in a small voice. "He didn't tell me." And here she'd wanted to kick Sam out. Out of the only home he'd ever known. "I'm allergic to cats," she murmured, as an explanation to her grandmother as much as anything.

"I'd gathered as much." Marie sipped her drink. "Hmm, good. So do the pills help?"

"Yeah, they do." Bonnie hadn't intended to take them after learning about Malloy, but then Sam had snuck into her part of the house again that day and in spite of her protests, had settled himself on her lap, purring like crazy. It had felt so good having the warmth of him cuddled against her, she'd endured the sneezes until he'd apparently got tired of hearing them and taken off. That's when she'd decided to begin taking the medicine.

"There's shots you can get once or twice a year, you know," Marie told her. "Might be less trouble."

Bonnie shuddered. "Needles give me the creeps." She laughed. "Just as well, I guess, since I lived on the streets and pushers—"

Appalled by her lapse, by what she'd inadvertently betrayed about herself, Bonnie snapped her mouth shut. Eyes wide and scared, she stared at Marie.

Only the merest flicker of lashes betrayed any surprise or shock Marie might have felt. The expression in her deep blue eyes didn't change; her gaze remained fixed on Bonnie's with genuine interest and warmth. "If you ever want to talk about it," she said, crossing her arms and settling back in her chair, "you'll find I'm a good listener."

Yeah, Bonnie thought, *but are you a talker, too?*

Caught in the other woman's kindly gaze, Bonnie felt ashamed of the wariness that caused her to doubt, to distrust, but old habits were hard to shake. She managed a careless shrug.

"There's nothing to say, really," she said, not looking Marie in the eye now. "One of those silly teenage things. You know. Something at home ticked me off and I split for a while." Forcing another little laugh, she slanted Marie a quick glance. "Dumb, huh?"

Marie shrugged, her expression bland so that Bonnie couldn't tell if her explanation had been swallowed or not. "Happens all the time," she said. "Half the kids at Saint C's are in that same boat."

"I know." Weak with relief, Bonnie latched onto the chance to steer the conversation into safer waters. "I went to see Father Joseph the other day, and he was telling me. I'm going to be teaching there a couple days a week," she added, just in case Marie thought she'd gone there for counseling.

"Teach?" This time there was no mistaking the surprise in the other woman's voice and facial expression. "You?"

Bonnie stiffened. "Why not me?" she asked, unable to quite keep resentment out of her voice.

Marie looked first chagrined, then sympathetic. She laid a hand over the fist Bonnie had unconsciously made. "Look, I'm sorry," she said earnestly. "I didn't mean to offend you. It's just that—"

She stopped speaking, moving her other hand in distress, but Bonnie could see in Marie's eyes the things the other woman hadn't yet said.

Dread made her go cold all over, and just as any animal who's cornered tends to attack, so Bonnie, too, took the offensive. She snatched her hand out from beneath Marie Donelly's and, with belligerence and hostility lacing her tones, demanded, "It's just that...*what?*"

For long moments Marie made no reply. Outside, the mower sputtered into silence, the sound replaced by birdsong and, now and then, Jennifer's hesitant soprano punctuating Frank Malloy's mellow baritone speech.

Bonnie heard it all, but at the same time, she heard nothing besides the thunderous beat of her heart. It seemed to stop dead, however, when Marie finally said, "It's just that I *know*, Bonnie. I know that you can't read."

Chapter Six

For several moments everything seemed suspended in a timeless vacuum. Bonnie could neither move nor in any way react to the words that had dropped like bombs into the peace she'd begun to find here in her grandmother's house. A peace that, she now knew, had been destined to be illusory and transient right from the start.

A person couldn't keep secret for long a shameful thing like the one she'd been carrying around. Not in a town this size, and not when, of necessity, certain of its citizens had had to be clued in. Like Linda, the teller at the savings and loan, and Father Joseph at Saint Christopher's....

No, the truth had been bound to come out. She'd expected to be caught a number of times, the first of which had been on the day she'd pretended to read Frank Malloy's lease. Upside down.

And yet now, faced with it, when at last she found her voice, Bonnie still couldn't admit it. Instead, her face scarlet and her hands balled into fists, she leapt to her feet. "That's a lie!" she exclaimed. "That's a dirty, rotten lie. I need glasses, that's all. Here, I'll show you—"

She rushed to the cupboard and snatched a dog-eared cookbook off a corner shelf. With trembling hands she randomly flipped it open, saying, "I'll just show you and then you'll see. Why, it says here..." Painstakingly, her voice roughened by emotions that were dangerously close to hysteria, Bonnie began to read. "'C-cut the sh-short, the shor-ten—'" A choked sob of frustration escaped her, the letters she was struggling to string together into a word blurred, but she doggedly tried again. "It says, 'cut the shor-te-ning in-to the f-f-flour until it re-resem—' Oh, *damn!*"

Furious with herself and with what she considered her stupidity, mortified because she'd just proved to Marie the thing she'd been so vehemently denying, Bonnie hurled the book across the kitchen. It struck the basement door before hitting the floor with a thump.

Bonnie buried her face in her hands. "Damn, damn, *damn!*" The word dripped self-loathing, and each repetition was punctuated with an anguished twisting of her torso from side to side.

"Oh, Bonnie..." Gently, Marie pulled Bonnie's hands away from her face. "Don't. Please, girl, don't do this. For crying out loud," she blustered when Bonnie kept averting her face, "Nobody can read when they don't have their glasses...."

Though Marie continued trying to get Bonnie to look at her, Bonnie kept her head bowed and shoulders slumped. "I lied about the glasses."

If Marie heard the admission, she chose to ignore it, because she went on talking just as if Bonnie hadn't spoken. "And it's not as if you have to prove anything to me," she said. "Or to anyone else, for that matter."

Yeah, right, Bonnie thought tiredly, and she almost wanted to laugh when she heard Marie say, "In any case, having trouble reading is nothing to be ashamed of. Why, I'm sure I heard or read somewhere that Einstein himself was a poor reader, and look at all he ended up doing."

Not caring in the least what some guy might have accomplished when her own dignity and pride hung in tatters, Bonnie nevertheless lifted her head. But she still didn't look at Marie.

"What?" she asked in a tone of defeat and indifference, her eyes fixed on a grease spot on the blue-and-white striped wallpaper above the stove. "What did he end up doing?"

"Well, you know." Marie's surprised little laugh made it clear that she figured Bonnie should've known all about it.

Bonnie mentally shrugged. Resentment began to override her feelings of shame. Hey, she thought, somehow they hadn't gotten around to him in the hit-and-miss sessions of school she'd attended, all right? Or maybe they had, but she'd been busy with more important stuff than listening. Like with catching some much needed shut-eye or dodging spitballs—when she wasn't firing them off herself.

She hadn't been called a goof-off for nothing; she'd earned the name. Teachers used to call her slow. Too slow to keep up with classwork, and too much trouble to spend extra time with. So they mostly ignored her—for which Bonnie had been profoundly grateful—and passed her along from grade to grade just to get rid of her.

So now she listened with lots of resentment and very little interest as Marie explained, "You know, *Albert* Einstein—$E = mc^2$, and all that. Atoms..." She met the dark frown Bonnie sent her with a helpless shrug. "I don't know, the man was a genius with math and physics and stuff. Really, really famous. Anyway, it doesn't matter, my point was that at one time he didn't read well, either."

"At twenty-one?" Bonnie challenged sarcastically.

"Well, no—"

"So when, then? Fifteen?"

"Well, I—"

"Ten? Younger? What, Marie?"

"I don't know. Younger. I think." Visibly uncomfortable beneath Bonnie's now relentless gaze, Marie shifted her own. "I think it might have been when he first started school."

"Right." Her tone and expression derisive, Bonnie went to pick the book up off the floor and not very gently shoved it back into its slot on the shelf. "In other words, your friend what's-his-name was nothing like me and you don't know the first damn thing about me or my problems."

"All right. Maybe I don't." Marie raised her eyes. "But look, Bonnie, I'm sorry—"

"Don't be." Bonnie stomped over to the sink and furiously began to wipe it.

"I'd like to help," Marie insisted. "If you want to talk about it—"

"I don't." Bonnie was scouring the greasy spot above the stove now.

"All right. But just let me tell you this. There're classes, tutors—"

Bonnie slammed down the sponge and whirled around. "Dammit, I know that, all right? I may be stupid, but I'm not ignorant, and I can certainly take care of my own problems."

No sooner had the bitter words been said than Bonnie fervently wished she could unsay them. How could she talk like that to a woman who was so obviously trying to be kind? After all, it wasn't as if she had so many friends she could afford to offend them. Besides which, having been on the receiving end of harsh words more often than she cared to remember, Bonnie hated to dish them out. She could tell she'd stepped on Marie's feelings.

"I'm sorry," Bonnie mumbled awkwardly, none too easy with apologies, received or given. One quick look at Marie eased her nervousness enough to manage a short, self-deprecating laugh. "I guess you can tell I'm touchy on the subject, huh?"

"I got that impression, yes." Humor tinged Marie's dry tone as she added, "And I guess you can tell I tend to get a mite pushy when I care about something."

"So did Ellie." Bonnie's small laugh sounded more natural this time.

"Ellie?"

"Eleanor Grimes." On a shiver of residual tension, Bonnie tightly hugged herself. "She pushed me into a lot of things I didn't think I wanted to do."

God, I wish she were here now.

The sudden thought brought with it such an acute stab of loneliness, tears blurred Bonnie's vision. She turned her head aside so Marie wouldn't see. "Ellie was my friend."

Marie touched her shoulder. "I'd hoped you and I could be friends, too, Bonnie."

"Did you?" Bonnie lifted her head. "Why?"

"Why...?" Marie repeated incredulously. "Because I like you."

"And because I need help?"

"We-e-l-l," Marie said carefully, searching Bonnie's expression with troubled eyes. "There's that, too, of course."

Pride asserted itself and Bonnie looked away. "Thanks, but I don't need any help."

"We all need help at one time or another," Marie said. She stepped away. "There's nothing wrong with that, and that's what friends are for."

"So they say," Bonnie said with a tentative smile.

"So I *know*." Marie smiled back and held out a hand. "Friends?"

Lips compressed to keep the lower one from wobbling, Bonnie nodded. "Friends."

To fill the somewhat awkward pause that followed, she picked up the pitcher of lemonade, now beaded with moisture. "More lemonade?"

At Marie's mute, negative headshake, Bonnie placed the pitcher into the refrigerator and keeping her tone deliberately bland and her back turned, screwed

NO RISK, NO OBLIGATION TO BUY . . . NOW OR EVER!

CASINO JUBILEE
"Scratch'n Match" Game

Here's how to play:

1. Peel off label from front cover. Place it in space provided at right. With a coin, carefully scratch off the silver box. This makes you eligible to receive two or more free books, and possibly other gifts, depending upon what is revealed beneath the scratch-off area.

2. You'll receive brand-new Silhouette Romance™ novels. When you return this card, we'll rush you the books and gifts you qualify for ABSOLUTELY FREE!

3. If we don't hear from you, every month we'll send you 6 additional novels to read and enjoy months before they are available in bookstores. You can return them and owe nothing but if you decide to keep them, you'll pay only $2.25* per book, a saving of 44¢ each off the cover price. There is **no** extra charge for postage and handling. There are **no** hidden extras.

4. When you join the Silhouette Reader Service™, you'll get our subscribers-only newsletter, as well as additional free gifts from time to time just for being a subscriber!

5. You must be completely satisfied. You may cancel at any time simply by sending us a note or a shipping statement marked ''cancel'' or by returning any shipment to us at our cost.

YOURS FREE!

> *This lovely heart-shaped box is richly detailed with cut-glass decorations, perfect for holding a precious memento or keepsake—and it's yours absolutely free when you accept our no-risk offer.*

© 1991 HARLEQUIN ENTERPRISES LIMITED.
*Terms and prices subject to change without notice.
Sales tax applicable in NY.

CASINO JUBILEE
"Scratch'n Match" Game

CHECK CLAIM CHART BELOW FOR YOUR FREE GIFTS!

YES! I have placed my label from the front cover in the space provided above and scratched off the silver box. Please send me all the gifts for which I qualify. I understand I am under no obligation to purchase any books, as explained on the opposite page.

(U-SIL-R-11/92) 215 CIS AGND

Name _____

Address _____ Apt. _____

City _____ State _____ Zip _____

CASINO JUBILEE CLAIM CHART

🍒🍒🍒	WORTH 4 FREE BOOKS, FREE HEART-SHAPED CURIO BOX PLUS MYSTERY BONUS GIFT	
🍒🔔🍒	WORTH 3 FREE BOOKS PLUS MYSTERY GIFT	
🔔🔔🍒	WORTH 2 FREE BOOKS	CLAIM N° 1528

◄ DETACH AND MAIL CARD TODAY! ►

SILHOUETTE ''NO RISK'' GUARANTEE

up her courage. "So, uh, so what did your brother have to say about it?"

"Say about what?"

Bonnie's heart, which until then had seemed to have lain like a lead weight in her chest, began to beat again. She slowly closed the refrigerator door, but stayed there.

"You know," she said, absently watching her hand slide up and down the smooth, worn handle. "About...everything. The drugstore and—and this..."

"You think I told him?"

Bonnie slowly turned. "You mean you didn't?"

Her heart beat a lot faster now, and its weight was almost back to normal.

"Would you have wanted me to?" Marie asked with eyebrows raised.

"God, no!" Bonnie closed her eyes, tight. Just the thought of Frank Malloy knowing was enough to make her sick to her stomach.

"You like my brother, don't you?"

Marie's softly voiced question made Bonnie's eyelids pop open right smart.

"And you know something," Marie added with a little smile, "I've got a feeling he likes you, too."

They looked at each other, Bonnie with skepticism and Marie grinning like the Cheshire Cat. "And you know what else?" she said after a bit.

Bonnie shook her head. She was too busy thinking, *Frank Malloy likes me?* to be able to speak.

But Marie didn't seem to expect a reply in any case. She returned to her chair and sat down, carefully crossing her legs and smoothing her skirt before slanting Bonnie an impish glance and saying, "I'm glad."

Oh, how Bonnie wished she were able to put into words the feelings that crowded her heart just then. Gratitude, joy, a rush of affection. But fear, too. Along with wariness. She needed to believe what Marie's words implied—that she'd welcome Bonnie as her brother's friend as well as her own—but she didn't quite dare. After all, how would Marie feel if she knew about the other things? About Bonnie's mother, for instance? Or about all the ugly, sordid things that had been part of Bonnie's childhood and that had, perhaps, warped her forever? What if Marie knew about those?

What if Frank knew? Another thought to turn her stomach.

Quickly, Bonnie shoved it away. Inhaling deeply, she returned Marie's smile, instilling her own with everything she couldn't find the words to say. The silence between them grew and might have become awkward with emotion had not the banging of a door, followed by heavy footsteps, interrupted it.

Bonnie's heart catapulted up into her throat and she spun toward the kitchen door just as it swung open.

Behind her, Marie Donelly chuckled delightedly.

Frank had tried to tell Jennifer that coming into Bonnie's kitchen for lemonade was not a good idea, but his little niece had been adamant. She'd grabbed his hand and literally dragged him into the house, all the while insisting that Bonnie had said he should come.

Fat chance, he thought, and the red-faced expression of alarm which his landlady displayed as he followed Jennifer into the kitchen did nothing to dispel his misgivings.

And what was it with his sister, sitting in Bonanza Coombs's kitchen, looking as smug as the D.A. after a landslide reelection? How did she happen to know Bonnie, anyway, and what was she doing here? He'd thought she and Jennifer had come to see *him*....

Slanting Marie a sour glance, he pried his fingers loose from Jennifer's. "Look, honey," he said, "I'd better go. I've got things to do and—"

"Oh, for Pete's sake, Frank," Marie said in an exasperated tone, "sit down. You, too, Jennifer." Then ignoring the frown her brother tossed her, she said to Bonanza, "Need help with those glasses, Bonnie?"

"Glasses ... ?" The situation had Bonnie rattled, and habit had her hand going up to check her face for spectacles.

"For the lemonade," Marie elaborated mildly.

"Oh." *Get a grip.* "No. Uh, thanks."

"U-Uncle F-Frank c-cut your g-grass for you, B-Bonnie," Jennifer announced, wiggling into position on the chair by the window.

"I know." Bonnie sent her a quick smile. "And it was very nice of him." She took the lemonade pitcher out of the refrigerator, aware that good manners dictated she say thanks to Frank now. She looked his way, reluctant to address him, and saw that he was pulling out the captain's chair at the head of the table.

Oh, no. The sketchbook.

Had she uttered the words aloud? As Frank sat down and three pairs of eyes the identical shade of blue swung questioningly toward her, Bonnie suspected she had.

She dredged up a feeble smile. "I'll take that," she told Frank who had already gotten off the chair again and was pulling the book out from under the cushion.

Though one of his eyebrows rose, indicating his surprise at this unlikely find, Frank obligingly handed her the book. But apprehension had tied the fingers of Bonnie's left hand in knots—her right was still holding the pitcher—and the book slid out of her grasp before she could properly get hold of it. It landed on the floor, two of its pages open for all to see.

Bonnie didn't need to see the head and face on the one page and the nude male study on the next to know she wanted to die of mortification. With another groan, she closed her eyes.

Staring down at the drawings, Frank's eyes widened with surprise and recognition—and so did Marie's. They exchanged a quick glance, and Frank flushed as Marie snickered. Jennifer was still craning her neck for a look when Frank scooped the thing up and snapped it closed.

"Why don't I put it on the shelf over here?" he said, his tone bland, though the eyes that met Bonnie's when at last she dared open them were anything but. They were alive with speculation and alight with a gleam that raised goose bumps on her arm.

Bonnie fervently wished that moment light-years away.

"I d-didn't g-get to see," Jennifer protested.

Bonnie was grateful for small mercies. "It was nothing," she said, risking a glance at Marie, who looked highly entertained. "Just some pictures I drew."

"And very well, too," Marie chimed in with considerable amusement. "Why, you're an artist, Bonnie Coombs. I had no idea."

Pouring lemonade, Bonnie flushed with pleasure in spite of her continued discomfiture. She kept feeling Frank Malloy's eyes on her like a physical touch. Oh, Lord—what was he thinking?

"I haven't really had any formal training," she explained nervously, handing Marie and Jennifer each a frosted glass, "but I do love to draw and paint. In fact, that's what I'll be doing at Saint Christopher's, teaching art."

She set a drink down in front of Frank and, finding herself on the receiving end of yet another of his penetrating stares, decided to take the bull by the horn right then and there rather than hang suspended until *he* decided to broach the subject that was on both their minds. Those sketches. It'd be much easier to clear up any misapprehensions he might have in front of others.

"Look, Officer Malloy—" she began, only to have him interrupt.

"I think we've progressed to Frank by now, don't you?" His eyes slid meaningfully to the shelf where she'd put the sketchbook.

Her face turning scarlet yet again, Bonnie decided to, for now, avoid names altogether. "I know what you must be thinking—"

"I doubt it."

He was as determined to fluster her as she was not to let him. Doggedly, Bonnie went on with what she

had to say. "I know that I had no right to draw you
without—"

"Clothes on?" he injected. "Oh, I don't know..."

"Without your permission." She sent him a fruitless, silencing look. "But you see, what really happened is that only—"

Frank kept right on talking. "...I just wish you'd
have let me have the pleasure of doing the actual posing. I've never been..."

"Only the face is you," Bonnie said. "I copied the
body out of an art book."

"...an artist's model before. It might have been
fun, you know, a novel expe—" Frank broke off,
frowning, as Bonnie's last statement belatedly sank in.
"Come again?"

"I said—" from behind her, Bonnie heard Marie
choke on her lemonade "—I copied the body..."

"Oh, really." Frank didn't believe her for a minute, mostly because he'd so thoroughly enjoyed the
idea of Bonnie preoccupied with his body. Day-
dreaming about it and lovingly sketching... Besides,
she looked too damn guilty to be innocent. His eyes
trapping hers told her so.

"Come on, Jennifer, time to go home," Marie de-
clared out of the blue, the scrape of her chair under-
scoring her words. "You can visit Bonnie and Uncle
Frank again another day. See you, guys."

Neither Frank nor Bonnie in any way acknowledged their departure. They were aware only of each
other. Though neither said any more, their gazes remained locked. All manner of wordless communica-
tion was going on.

Vibrations so strong as to almost be tactile bounced back and forth in the charged air between them, which like a force field, held both of them in place. Heat, too—*body heat*—was palpably being exchanged by virtue of their proximity to each other—Frank seated in the captain's chair and Bonnie standing so near his left thigh, the merest movement to the right would have her own brushing against it. With each rapidly accelerating breath, they inhaled each other's scent.

Bonnie discovered dark flecks in the crystalline clarity of Frank's blue eyes, as well as a whole range of emotions that made her heart trip over itself and her pulses gallop. Something began to tingle deep down inside her, something every bit as hot and heavy as the air felt between them just then. But exciting—oh, so much more exciting.

She saw Frank's pupils widen, darken, and she wondered if what she felt was reflected in her gaze, as well.

It was.

And Frank's body responded to that message the way male bodies had responded to the lure of women since the dawn of time. With passion, hot and urgent. So urgent that, without conscious thought, without regard for consequences, Frank reached out and hauled Bonanza into his lap.

In one smooth movement, her soft, slender body tumbled gracefully onto his hardening one, and her head came to rest against his shoulder just right. Luscious lips, rounded in a silent O of surprise, were only a breath away. Their softness beckoned and, without hesitation, Frank responded. Fully. Hotly. Deeply.

He felt Bonnie stiffen and, with a moan that was as much from unfulfilled need as from regret, he prepared to let her go. But before he could, she relaxed. More, she grew ardent. She melted into him with a small sound of surrender, opening her lips and taking in his tongue.

For just an instant, it seemed to Frank that heaven was near. Bonnie's mouth was warm, willing and, oh, so sweet. Her tongue, smooth as satin, shyly touched his. Pleasure suffused his body—just a pulse beat before a sharp pain made him gasp and rear back. In his mouth, the sweet taste of Bonnie was replaced by the coppery taste of blood.

"You bit me!"

Bonnie barely heard the incredulous exclamation. Every survival instinct she possessed urged her out of those arms, off that lap and as far away from the man as possible. At the door to the basement, she spun to face him with both arms hugging her midsection.

Frank opened his mouth to repeat his accusation, but one look at Bonnie's ghost white face and fear-filled eyes had him close it again. When she neither moved nor spoke, though, but only stared at him as if at a dangerous criminal, he ventured a tentative, "Bonnie?"

The soft call of her name was like the brush of velvet against Bonnie's eardrums. It made her shiver, and she hugged herself more tightly.

"You—you shouldn't have done that," she whispered hoarsely. "You had no right to do that."

"Do what? Kiss you?" Injured masculine pride was momentarily blinding Frank to the fact that Bonnie's words were merely an inadequate expression of some deep seated horror and fear.

"Hell, you wanted it as much as I did. Don't deny it," he insisted heatedly, surging to his feet and striding toward her as she just kept mutely shaking her head.

Frank's flushed face, his purposeful movement toward her were to Bonnie like scenes from the past. As she stood, rooted, and watched him come closer, Frank's features blurred and were replaced by the malevolent countenance of Sheriff Claymore.

He was almost upon her, one hand at his belt, the other raised to strike.

Bonnie jerked back against the basement door, both of her arms raised to shield her face. "Don't," she whimpered. "Don't hit me. Please—"

"Hit you?" Thunderstruck, horrified, Frank stood in front of the cowering Bonanza. "My God, Bonnie, you can't believe I'd..." Words failed him when, as he gently tried to pry her arms away from her face, she flinched and protectively curled into herself.

And then a white-hot fury literally made him see red. Who had done this to her? Who was the swine who had used and abused Bonanza Coombs so that a simple kiss, honest passion, had become something to be feared, to shrink from? Who had *dared* to beat her?

The answer, when it hit him, caused nausea to rise to his throat.

A policeman, that's who.

Chapter Seven

Huddled against the wall, Bonnie heard the kitchen door clicking shut as from a distance. It sounded to her like the clang of a jail-cell door locking her into the horror within. She stayed as she was, unmoving, as the footsteps slowly receded and stairs creaked beneath a heavy tread. It wasn't until she heard yet another door, an upstairs door, shut that she moved. But all she did then was to slowly slide down the wall until she was crouched on the floor.

There she stayed, curled in a tight little ball, as if to forcibly keep the nightmare inside from escaping.

It was the touch of his tongue that had done it, she thought. It had filled her mouth, though the sensation—this time—had at first not been unpleasant.

But then, suddenly, it hadn't been *this time*. It had been that other, horrible time. It had been *then*.

It had been old Claymore's lap she'd been imprisoned on. It had been old Claymore's hands touching and stroking and holding her in place. It had been old Claymore's tongue—

In a flash, horror, disgust, panic had wiped out the sweet feelings of moments before. All she'd been able to think— No, she hadn't *thought*, had only acted. Run, her brain had ordered, supplying the adrenaline she'd need to escape the clutch of that much bigger, much stronger man.

But she hadn't escaped him for long.

Claymore had come after her and, as she'd cowered against the trunk of a tree, he'd taken his belt and beat her. Later, when he'd delivered her bruised and battered into the hands of the authorities, he told them her mother had done it.

By then Bonanza had learned that it didn't pay to protest. The word of Loretta Coombs's bastard daughter meant nothing against the word of the law.

When Bonnie finally roused herself from her waking nightmare, she had no idea how much time had passed. All she knew was that she ached all over, as if the events of the past she'd just relived had occurred in reality, too. Moving stiffly, stifling groans of bone-deep pain, she struggled to her feet. With dragging steps, she walked out of the kitchen and across the hall into her bedroom. Dropping onto the bed, she slept.

When Bonnie awoke, the room was dark. She didn't know what time it was, but she didn't care enough to glance at the bedside clock radio and find out. She was hungry, but, again, not enough to rouse herself from the languor that was holding her in a state of suspended animation. She shivered, cold in her shorts and skimpy top, but she didn't get up to slide under the covers, either. She just reached out a hand, found a handful of quilted bedspread and pulled it over herself.

She did it all automatically, without conscious volition. Her thoughts were still focused inward, though they were no longer mired in the morass of her past. They were centered on Frank Malloy and on what had happened between them in the kitchen *before* her emotions had run amok.

Lying in the darkness with no one to see her, Bonnie allowed herself to examine and savor the feelings Frank had stirred in her. They had been good feelings. Though they had been new to her, and more exciting than she ever would have dreamed, she hadn't been afraid. She had welcomed them. Being close to Frank, feeling his strength and absorbing his warmth had been like finding nourishment after a long fast. She had wanted it, wanted to be where she was, and had tried to give back some of the sweet things he was making her feel.

She hadn't thought of him as a policeman. She had spared no thought for the fact that he was her tenant, that she'd been mortified at having him see her sketches or for any of the many other little grievances she'd been hoarding and stacking into a wall of defenses against the attraction that had been pulling her toward him even as she'd struggled to stay clear.

All she'd thought of in that endless moment during which their gazes had seemed to search each other's soul and her heart had raced were the wondrous sensations that had flooded her. Sensations that had culminated in a graceful tumble onto his lap and an eager meeting of his lips with hers.

He'd been gentle, and, though only for a very short time, his passion had kindled her own.

Above Bonnie's head, the ceiling creaked, telling her that Frank was awake, too, and walking around. Bonnie recalled then the horrible moment of their parting, and it suddenly occurred to her that she might well have wounded Frank deeply with her behavior. He had no way of knowing her reaction hadn't been brought about through any fault of his own. He hadn't meant to hurt her, and Bonnie—the rational Bonnie of here and now—knew that with certainty.

Was he blaming himself? Was she the reason he was sleepless and pacing? Suddenly it became imperative that she tell him he wasn't to blame.

No longer relaxed and languid, but infused with purpose, Bonnie tossed back the spread and leapt off the bed. She was out the door and through the hall before second thoughts had a chance to question the wisdom of her actions. She rushed up the stairs and knocked on Frank's door.

It opened so fast, Frank might have been standing on the other side of it, waiting for her.

"What the hell— Bonanza!" Frank searched her pale face, then looked beyond her into the stairwell and the foyer below. "What's the matter? What's wrong? Anything wrong?"

Bonnie shook her head, struck for a moment by a case of nerves and the sight of dark and curling chest hair at eye level. Frank was wearing a short, pale blue terry cloth kimono, which exposed his chest in a tantalizing V.

"Umm . . ." Nervously, Bonnie cleared her throat. "Can I come in?"

"Sure. Sure." Bewildered, worried, Frank stepped aside. "You okay?" he asked with another sharp scan of the stairs and hall. Everything looked normal. Bonnie, though clearly perturbed about something, seemed physically unharmed. A bit warily—their last encounter had left some scars—he closed the door. Leaning against it, he shoved his hands into his pockets.

"Okay, you're in." He'd decided in the course of this wakeful night to let the lady set the pace and tone between them from now on.

Bonnie walked farther into the living room, then turned to face him. "You're mad at me," she said, and when he would have interrupted with a brusque denial, she rushed on. "And I don't blame you. I came to . . ."

Why was it always so damn hard to apologize? Bonnie swallowed and tried again. "I'm sorry, that's what I came to say."

"*You're* sorry?" Frank shoved away from the door and strode over to her. Forgetting his intentions, he gripped her shoulders. "Good God, Bonanza, you've got nothing to be sorry about."

"But—"

"If anything, *I'm* the one who should apologize." He hauled her against his chest, pressed his cheek to her hair. "Lord, but I'm so sorry. . . ."

"Don't, Frank. Please. It wasn't you."

"It was a cop." He hugged her tighter. "It's the same thing."

"No." Bonnie strained against his hold. When he loosened his embrace, she looked into his face. "For a little while, that's what I thought, but I don't anymore."

"Who?" Frank's eyes burned into hers. "Who was it, Bonanza?"

"It doesn't matter." She tried to avert her eyes, but Frank wouldn't let her.

He caught her chin. "It does matter, don't you see that? It matters a hell of a lot. To me, if not to you."

Helplessly trapped in the fiery intensity of Frank's gaze, Bonnie licked dry lips and mutely stared back.

Frank gentled his grip. "I need to know, Bonanza," he said quietly. "Please. Tell me."

Tell him?

"No." The idea was so repulsive, it made Bonnie's feet itch to run and had her twisting her head from side to side in an effort to be free. When Frank refused to release her, panic surged.

"Let go of me!" She violently wrenched out of his hold. "I don't have to tell you anything. I owe you nothing. I only came up here to say it wasn't your fault." She moved toward the door. "I've said it, okay? And I'm going."

"Was it someone at Whitworth, Bon?"

Frank's soft-spoken question stopped her as surely as if he'd yanked on a tether. She felt the blood drain out of her face and take with it all the heat in her body. A shiver ran down her spine.

"How..." She swallowed. "How do you know about Whitworth?"

Frank ignored the question, coming back with another of his own. "Or was it before that? Like when they hauled you in off the streets? Or when you ripped off Jersey's Market in Irvine, or the time you ran without paying out of Calloni's Pizza Emporium in Portland, Oregon?''

''I was hungry.'' Bonnie didn't turn around, and she spoke automatically. Her eyes were fixed unblinkingly on the white-semigloss-enamel expanse of Frank Malloy's apartment door.

He knew everything.

''And, no, it wasn't any of those times. Or at least, not the worst of it.''

She didn't ask how Frank knew about the things he knew. No longer wondered. Wasn't he a cop?

''You mean it was before?'' The horrifying implication of his dawning realization made Frank feel physically ill.

''I was ten.''

Ten. Christ! Frank let go a string of vicious curses. *Just a couple of years older than Jennifer.*

Needing to hit something, he slapped an open palm against the nearest wall. His prized set of framed watercolors bucked once and slid out of alignment. ''Did he—''

''Rape me?'' Bonnie looked down, closed her eyes. ''I guess that depends. Technically, physically, not—not completely. But inside—'' She bit her lip with a violent shake of the head. After a moment she said brokenly, ''I don't want to talk about it anymore, okay?''

But Frank couldn't let it go yet. He had to know. ''Who was it, Bonanza?''

Inside Bonnie something snapped. Her head jerked up. ''You mean there's something you don't know?''

she snarled. "You mean you've dug up every other piece of dirt you could lay your hands on and still you don't *know?* What's the matter, Officer Malloy, wouldn't your *sources*—that's what you call your network of stool pigeons, isn't it?—wouldn't they come clean about the name? Why is that, do you s'pose? Huh?"

She was furious. Tears were streaming down her face, but Frank was sure Bonnie wasn't even aware of them. She was caught up in her rage, directing it at him, but in his gut Frank knew her attack wasn't personal so much as a tirade—perhaps long overdue—against a system that she felt had cruelly let her down.

And so he stood and took what she dished out, silent, and hurting. Hurting for her.

"What?" Bonnie jeered. "Nothing to say, Officer Malloy? Not that I'm surprised. None of you cops have anything to say when one of your own steps out of line, do you? Stick together and keep your traps shut, isn't that how it goes? Turn a blind eye and lie through your teeth. Who'd believe the ten-year-old daughter of a whore anyway, right?"

She stepped up to him then, hips swaying, eyes cold as ice, mouth curving in a seductive smile, and playfully let her fingers walk along the exposed V of his chest. "Would you have believed me, Frankie?" she purred. "Hmm?"

"Don't." Frank caught her wrists and pulled her hands away. "It wasn't me, Bonanza. And it wasn't anybody I know. So don't do this. It's over."

"Is it?" Bonnie's smile turned crooked, quivered. The coldness in her eyes was replaced by such sadness; Frank knew again the urge to do physical dam-

age to something. Some*one*. Remnants of tears made
Bonnie's huge hazel eyes shimmer golden-green as she
whispered, "Is it over, Frank?"

He hesitated, then thought, the hell with it. Word-
lessly, he put her hands back against his chest and
pulled her close. He wrapped his arms around her and
laid his chin on the crown of the head, which, with a
choked little sob, she let drop to his shoulder.

And he stood like a rock, solid and unmoving,
holding Bonanza and keeping her safe while years and
years of accumulated grief at last found release in a
torrent of tears.

When, a couple of days later, Marie Donelly phoned
to invite Bonanza to dinner at the home she shared
with her parents, Bonnie's first reaction was panic and
a resounding and not very tactful, "No!"

What if Frank were to be there? she thought, cring-
ing at the recollection of the other night. After she'd
so thoroughly lost it up in his apartment, he'd carried
her downstairs and put her to bed, for cripes' sake. Put
her to bed and patted her to sleep just as if she were
some helpless little baby—or some hysterical female
who'd worn herself out.

Bonnie didn't know which of the two was worse, but
she did know it'd be quite a while before she could
look Frank Malloy in the eye again. And not just because of the crying, either, but because now he knew
all her secrets.

Well, almost all.

He knew about her sordid past; he knew that she
was tainted, sullied. She'd seen the horror on his face;
she wouldn't be able to bear seeing disgust there, too.

And what if he told Marie? Or, heaven forbid, his parents?

But deep inside she knew he wouldn't.

"I'm not taking no for an answer, Bonnie." With gentle authority, Marie cut short Bonnie's agonizing. "Jennifer is really looking forward to it."

"That's blackmail," Bonnie said, weakening.

"I know." Marie sounded smug. "Whatever works. It's time you met some people, don't you think?"

"I s'pose." But Frank Malloy's parents? "Is, uh, will Frank...?"

"Sorry, no. Last I heard, he's working a split shift."

Marie's chuckle had driven heat into Bonnie's face, but, darn it, she hadn't been dodging him here at home for two days just to come unexpectedly face-to-face with him at his parents' house.

"All right, I'll come."

Bonnie remembered some of Ellie's instructions in time to stop at Miller's market and buy a bouquet of flowers to give to Mrs. Malloy. Carnations. She chose pink ones. They came already bundled into a bunch with a couple of twigs of baby's breath for softness and a stalk of fern for contrast. They were wrapped in cellophane.

"I love carnations, don't you?" Florence Jackson at the checkstand was her usual cordial self. She always had something nice to say to Bonnie. "Are they for yourself?"

"No." Not sure what else to confide and unable to come up with some bit of small talk the way Ellie, no doubt, would have, Bonnie fumbled with her purse.

"Oh? So they're a gift then," Florence went on undaunted. "Want me to wrap them in some pretty paper for you?"

Bonnie looked up in surprise. "Would you?"

"Sure, hon." Florence ducked down beneath the counter and came up with a nice floral wrap. "It's slow today, I'd be glad to. How's this?"

"Very nice. Thank you."

"Bet you can draw prettier designs than that, though, huh?" Florence said, deftly wrapping. At Bonnie's small frown of inquiry, she smiled. "My Lester's in the class you taught at Saint C's yesterday. He told me all about you. Said he can't hardly wait till next week 'cause you said you'd show the kids how to make a kite."

"Really?" Pleasure suffused Bonnie's face in a warm glow. "Which one is Lester? There's fifteen kids," she hastened to explain apologetically. "It's hard to remember them all the first day."

"'Course it is." With a flourish, Florence tied a neat bow in a piece of red ribbon and attached it. "He's the towhead with no front teeth...."

"Oh, sure. I remember him."

"Bet you do. He's a wiggler. Teachers generally know him right quick 'cause he drives them crazy."

"I don't mind." Bonnie smiled. "I used to be a wiggler myself. No, the reason I remember him is because he did some pretty fine artwork. He likes airplanes."

"That's all he ever draws."

"Says he wants to be a pilot like his dad."

"Yeah." Florence's smile fled. She held the wrapped bouquet out to Bonnie. "Here you go. That'll be four thirty-eight with tax."

What had she said? Troubled by the change in Florence and quick to blame herself for it, Bonnie awkwardly fumbled for the money.

"We're divorced," Florence said, and Bonnie's head came up again. "Lester and I moved here from Atlanta a year ago, but he still misses his daddy. That's why he goes to Saint C's twice a week. Between Father Joe and Detective Malloy, he's at least getting *some* manly input."

Funny how her heart jumped at the mention of Detective Malloy, Bonnie thought. Funny how she instantly saw him in her mind's eye and how what she saw made her mouth go dry.

"'Course you know Frank Malloy," Florence went on, "I don't have to tell you what a great guy he is."

Unaccountably, something like pride made Bonnie glow. "He's my tenant," she said, and she couldn't quite stifle the little note of possessiveness in her voice or the feeling in her chest.

"I know." Florence handed Bonnie change from a five. "Lester just loves him. Don't you?"

Did she? Bonnie wrestled with the answer to Florence's question off and on all the while she was walking to the Malloy's house. At first it almost made her laugh. If the woman only knew, she thought. Love, as it pertained to Malloy and herself, was not and never would be in the picture. Strangely, though, the longer she thought about it, the less it amused her.

She liked him. And, truth to tell, she probably could quite easily love him. The trouble was, with everything he knew about her and—just as bad—everything he didn't, she doubted he'd ever be able to love *her*.

Oh, he was kind. And he felt bad for her, she knew that. Especially since it was a policeman who'd hurt her. And he felt a little responsible for her, especially since Addie—her grandmother—had been his friend. But love?

With a heavy heart and the greatest reluctance, Bonnie pushed open the gate in the white picket fence that enclosed the yard of 1368 Alder. Marie had given her the address, and Bonnie had painstakingly written it down. Her skills were improving daily.

Her spirits rose when, with an exclamation of joy, little Jennifer bounded down the porch steps toward her.

"B-Bonnie! You c-came!"

"Wouldn't miss it," Bonnie said jauntily, taking the little girl's hand.

She turned when a male voice, reminiscent in tone of a younger version she'd gotten to know quite well in the past few weeks, warmly said, "That's about as excited as I've seen this young lady in a long time. You must be very special."

Bonnie flushed hotly then, and nervously smiled. The eyes meeting hers were yet another edition of the one's that had followed her into her dreams these past couple of nights. There were other similarities, too. The full shock of hair, though this one was amply laced with gray. The cleft in the chin.

"Frank Malloy, Senior," the man said, and his twinkle was purely Frank, Junior, too.

"Hi," Bonnie returned, feeling shy and awkward as she clung to Jennifer's little hand, at the same time trying to shift her bouquet so that she could shake the hand Frank, Senior, was extending to her. "I'm Bonanza Coombs."

"Glad to know you," he said, and amused by her dilemma, added, "D'you want me to hold those for you?"

"Would you?" She handed him the flowers, then shook his free hand. "I'm glad to know you, too." And then she took the flowers back. "These are for your wife."

"Oh." Frank, Senior's, lips twitched. "Well, let's go find her, shall we? She'll be in the kitchen, cooking up a storm. Nothing Darlene loves better than another mouth to feed. Hope you're hungry...."

Bonnie was curious more than hungry. Curious to see the house in which Frank Malloy had grown up, and curious about the woman who had raised him. Led by Jennifer, still holding her hand, Bonnie followed Frank, Senior, across a shaded screened porch into a cool living room.

Clutter. A riot of colors in upholstery print; a jungle of houseplants. Two fish tanks. People photos everywhere. Ditto crocheted doilies, knickknacks and books. Snowy starched curtains.

Warmth. Security. The feelings embraced Bonnie like the arms of a lover.

She stood still and basked in them. She closed her eyes and thought she could hear children's laughter and fires crackling in the hearth beneath the mantel

crowded with bric-a-brac. She thought she could hear
a babble of animated conversation and childish fingers making painstaking music on the old upright piano that sat along one wall. She imagined the sounds
of running feet and gentle scolding and stories read
aloud at bedtime . . .

Why couldn't she have grown up in a home like
this? Or at least have been fostered in one where there
was a sense of family and love such as this, she
thought with an ache in her heart.

But then a sense of fairness had her thinking, maybe
she had been, only she'd been too messed up and angry in those days to know it.

"Bonnie?" Marie was gently touching her shoulder. Bonnie reluctantly opened her eyes. "Are you all
right?" A small frown of concern puckered Marie's
brow. "Pops came into the kitchen still talking to you,
but you weren't there."

Bonnie smiled. "I'm fine." Her gaze once more
swept the room. "This is so . . . so *homey.*"

Marie looked around, too. "What this is," she
countered wryly, "is a mess. Mom can't bear to toss
out anything one of us ever made, and every picture
ever taken just *has* to be on display. I mean, look at
this one. . . ."

She took a framed photo from the piano. "I'm fifteen, fat and freckled, and Frankie had just dumped
a pail of water over my head. See, there he is with the
bucket still in his hand. Our brother Robbie's the kid
you see running away in the corner there. . . ."

But Bonnie wasn't looking at Robbie. Nor did she
spare the drenched and outraged Marie more than a
cursory glance before her gaze latched onto Frank. At

seventeen or so, his physique wasn't quite as impressive and powerful as it had grown with maturity, still in nothing but cutoff jeans and a what-the-hell smile, he seemed to Bonnie's fascinated gaze a most handsome and appealing young man.

"I never had a brother," she said softly, regretfully.

Marie chuckled. "That day I would've gladly given you mine. There's times I still would."

And I'd gladly take him.

"Well, for gosh sakes, there you are!" An authoritative female voice sounded from behind them, startling Bonnie and bringing a guilty expression to Marie's face. "Marie Malloy, what's the matter with you, keeping our guest standing here when dinner's nearly on the table and I haven't even met her yet? Hello," the woman continued without pause, giving Bonnie a quick but thorough once-over. She must've been pleased by what she saw, because a smile now lightened her stern countenance, making her look remarkably like Jennifer. She wiped a hand on her floral-print apron and held it out. "So you're the California girl. Welcome."

"Bonnie, meet my mother, Darlene Malloy," Marie said, looking from one woman to the other with amused interest. "She's been dying to meet you."

"Oh, hush," Darlene blustered. The flush that pinked her cheeks instantly endeared her to Bonnie and put her at ease.

"I've been looking forward to meeting you, too," Bonnie said warmly, no longer feeling the least bit awkward. She shook Darlene's hand, then offered the wrapped bouquet. "I brought you flowers."

"Oh, how thoughtful of you. And how pretty this paper is!" Darlene carefully removed the ribbon and wrap. "It's too good to throw away," she said, "I'll save it and the ribbon, too."

Marie shot Bonnie a mischievous see-what-I-mean glance, and Bonnie smiled. She was warmed and gratified by Frank's mother's reception of her and of her small gift, and pleased as punch with herself for having thought to bring it.

"Oh!" Darlene exclaimed. "Carnations. How lovely. Thank you, Bonanza." And before Bonnie could fathom her intent, Frank's mother enfolded her in a hug and kissed her on the cheek.

Darlene smelled of cinnamon and apples, and Bonnie would have liked to rest in her embrace for longer than the occasion and their short acquaintance allowed. She felt drawn to this woman who was Frank Malloy's mother; she felt good with her.

Dinner was eaten in the kitchen, family style. It was a lively affair. The food—chicken and dumplings, with homegrown tossed greens, homemade bread and apple cobbler for dessert—was delicious. Everybody talked at once and about every conceivable topic, and since they seemed to take it for granted that Bonnie would chime right in, she did. Only Jennifer sat silent, though her eyes lit up whenever they settled on Bonnie.

"She's really taken a shine to you," Marie whispered to Bonnie after the elder Malloys had gone to sit on the porch and the three of them—Marie, Bonnie and Jennifer—cleaned up the kitchen and dishes after the meal.

"The feeling's mutual," Bonnie said, exchanging a smile with Jennifer as she came back inside from shaking out the tablecloth. "Jennifer promised to show me her room," Bonnie went on in a louder tone, "just as soon as we're done here. Didn't you, Jen?"

Jennifer nodded. "C-can you s-stay a l-long t-time?"

"Long enough to see all your stuff, that's for sure." Bonnie handed her a dried plate to put away in the cupboard.

"A-and can—can you read me a s-story?"

Bonnie's cheeks heated. She exchanged a quick look with Marie, who gave a wry half shrug and remained silent.

"Sure," Bonnie said heartily, though her heart beat with dread. What if she couldn't do it? "Or we could color," she added hopefully.

"We c-could, we could d-draw p-pictures...." Jennifer was quick to expand on Bonnie's suggestion. "Y-you c-could show m-me how to d-draw Uncle F-Frankie...."

Marie burst out laughing, and Bonnie flushed scarlet, but when, a little later, she and Jennifer were in the little girl's room, it wasn't Frank they ended up discussing. It was Jennifer's father.

Though his framed portrait was prominently positioned on the nightstand, Jennifer didn't show it to Bonnie until the very last.

"T-this is m-m-my d-d-daddy," she said, in the first stutter Bonnie had heard from her since they'd come into the room. "H-his n-name is M-M-Michael D-Do—"

"Michael Donelly," Bonnie inserted smoothly. "What a nice name." She took the photo Jennifer held out and studied it with care. "Isn't he handsome? Look at that smile. Why—" She narrowed her eyes and looked assessingly from the picture to Jennifer and back. "I *know* where I've seen that smile before! It's yours, isn't it, you lucky girl. Your daddy gave you his smile to keep forever and ever. I think that's wonderful, don't you?"

She hugged Jennifer tightly when the little girl's eyes clouded with loss. "Say, did you ever hear the story of the hand-me-down smile?" she asked softly, talking into the child's silky hair, inhaling and savoring its baby-sweet scent. At Jennifer's negative shake of the head, Bonnie added, "It's not a very long story—" she was making things up as she went "—but it's always been one of my favorites. It's about this angel, see. He's sitting up on a cloud, brushing his wings and keeping an eye on things down on Earth—"

"What's his name?" Jennifer whispered without stumbling once over the words.

Bonnie swallowed a rush of emotion and gave the little body in her arms a quick squeeze. "Oh, didn't I say?" she asked with mock surprise. "His name is Michael."

"Same as my daddy's."

"Hey, so it is! Well, anyway, Angel Mikey—that's what they call him there—is on smile patrol this day. He's got a big book on his lap with everybody's name in it, and he keeps track of all the smiles in the world, who's got them and how often are they used. You see," she explained to Jennifer, who had drawn away now—though only far enough so she could look into

Bonnie's face as, spellbound, she listened, "you see, smiles are special gifts, and they have to be taken good care of. People have to use them often—"

"Even if they don't feel like it?"

"*Especially* when they don't feel like it, because, you see, smiles are magic, too. When you give one away, you get many more back, and then, suddenly, you feel good all over. But we're getting sidetracked here. As I was saying, Michael was up on his cloud—"

A movement at the door made Bonnie glance sharply, self-consciously, in that direction, and the words got stuck in her throat.

Frank.

His eyes met Bonnie's startled gaze with an expression unlike any Bonnie had seen in them before. Heat, hunger, puzzlement and wonder...

In response, Bonnie felt a rush of blood swirl tinglingly through her heart before it pooled in a fiery eddy in the pit of her stomach.

"I didn't mean to intrude," Frank said.

"Uncle Frank!" Jennifer raced toward him and shrieked with delight when he scooped her up and swung her high. "B-Bonnie is t-telling me a s-story," she told him excitedly when he'd set her back down, his gaze all the while holding Bonnie's. "And—and I've g-got m-my d-daddy's smile and I—I have to t-take good c-care of it...."

"I thought you were working a swing shift," Bonnie said, flustered by his presence, by the way he kept looking at her and by the crazy mixture of happiness and apprehension that was making her insides churn.

"I am. I'm on a break."

"Oh." She hadn't wanted to see him, had been afraid to. So how come she felt so totally happy?

"I had no idea you'd be here," he said.

Did he mean he wished she weren't? The pleasure of seeing him ebbed. Bonnie frowned. "Likewise."

Was she implying she wouldn't have come otherwise? Frank frowned, too. "Well, like I said, I didn't mean to intrude."

"You didn't." But he had, and he'd broken the mood. There was no way she'd be able to come up with any more story, not that Jennifer seemed to want to hear, anyway, now that her adored uncle was there.

Bonnie got up from the low stool on which she'd been perched. "I've got to get home."

"Why?" This from Frank and Jennifer in unison.

"Y-you d-didn't draw m-me a p-picture," Jenny added pleadingly.

Bonnie gave her a smile. "We'll draw another time."

"W-when?"

"Anytime you want."

"T-tomorrow?"

"If it's okay with your mom."

"I'll ask her." So saying, Jennifer rushed off, leaving Bonnie and Frank face-to-face. And alone.

Chapter Eight

"You're great with the kid," Frank finally said into the pregnant silence that had fallen after Jennifer's departure. "I've never seen her take to anyone the way she took to you right off the bat."

"I like kids. I guess..." Bonnie wished he weren't so close; her pulse rate and body temperature were rising fast. Yet she didn't want to be the one to move away. God forbid he should realize how much his nearness disturbed her. "I guess they sense that or something. I used to work in a day-care center before I moved here."

"Really?" Only half of Frank's mind was on their conversation, the other was eagerly taking stock of Bonnie's finely boned features, the sweep of her eyebrows, the curve of her lips. And he remembered how soft, warm and sweet they'd been.

Beneath Frank's avid gaze, Bonnie felt her lips go dry. She would have liked to moisten them, but instinct told her this was not a good time. Needing to do something, she sucked her lower lip between her teeth, and then she tried to get out of the line of fire.

"Excuse me," she murmured, moving ahead and sideways a little as an indication to Frank that he was blocking the door and she wanted to pass. But Frank didn't move, and all she accomplished was to be even closer to him. "I need to go home," she said.

"I'll drive you."

"No, thanks. I like to walk." She tried to edge past him.

He didn't budge. "Tell me something," he said. "Do you ever go out?"

Surprise at the question overcame nervousness. Bonnie drew back a bit and looked at him. "You mean go out as in date?"

"Yeah."

"No."

"Would you like to?"

Nervousness rushed back triplefold. "I . . ."

What was he saying? *You know what he's saying, Bonanza.* Don't be ridiculous . . . him, go out with me?

She swallowed. "With who?"

Frank's mouth curved into a funny little smile that made Bonnie's knees go weak. He lifted his hand and gently cupped her cheek. "Who do you think, Bonanza? With me."

Her eyelids fluttered and, for just a moment, she savored the feel of his callused palm on her face. But she opened her eyes and drew away almost instantly. She frowned and tried desperately to slow her racing heart. And she tried to hush the voice inside that urged, Say yes. Say yes. Say yes.

"Why?"

Frank looked at her mouth for a long time before he lifted his gaze to hers. "Because," he said huskily, "I very much want to."

And going out with you, I find, is only the half of what I want, he added silently.

"Why?" Bonnie repeated, wanting to say yes, but afraid. She couldn't have said of what—after all, she had no more secrets to keep from Frank. Well, almost none. And she could no longer be bothered to deny that she...liked him. Very much. "Where would we go?"

"Anywhere you want."

"*When* would we go?"

"You name it. Tomorrow night? Take in a movie maybe? Or on Sunday—I'm off on Sunday—we could go for a drive. Have you been to Olympia? Seen the capitol?"

"Umm...yeah." She went to Olympia every Thursday night for her reading sessions with Jack Trainer, her literacy tutor. But she wasn't about to tell Frank *that*. "Yeah, I've been to Olympia."

"So how about Ocean Shores? You been there?"

"I love the ocean."

"All *right!*" Deciding it was best to take her remark as an affirmative answer to his invitation and not give her a chance to renege, Frank beamed. Relaxing suddenly, he stepped aside and, as Bonnie came through the door, draped a companionable arm across her shoulders. Keep it cool, he warned himself. Don't rush her.

"Tell you what we'll do," he said, walking her up the hall and through the living room toward the porch. "You fix a picnic and we'll make a day of it...."

Sunday dawned cloudless and warm. In a few short hours, the day would become a scorcher. Where better to spend it than at the beach?

Once Olympia was behind them, everything was—for Bonnie—new territory. She looked around eagerly as they drove west to Aberdeen and Hoquiam, and out onto the peninsula of Grays Harbor.

It was green. Everywhere she looked, trees and shrubs in various shades of green abounded—pines and hemlocks, alder, maple and birch. Scotch broom, no longer in bloom. When it came to identifying the flora and fauna, Frank proved to be every bit as knowledgeable as Ellie had been. Bonnie's enthusiasm clearly pleased him. As he drove, they talked easily of this and that, and the last remnants of whatever misgivings Bonnie might have had about this date were left behind somewhere along Route 12.

At Ocean Shores, the wide, wide stretch of sandy beach was something else to astound her. And though many people besides them had apparently decided to leave the heat of the city behind, Frank managed to find a fairly empty spot on the beach for their picnic. They weren't hungry yet, but a walk along the fringe of the surf sounded good.

Bonnie had bought a new swimsuit for the occasion, a brightly hued maillot, since she thought her California bikinis just a bit too bare. She disregarded the fact that in California that self-same bareness hadn't bothered her in the least. She'd put it on at home already, beneath khaki walking shorts and a white T-shirt, and now she stepped out of them before they set out on their walk.

She did so with unselfconscious grace, all her faculties engaged by the goings-on around her, and her thoughts on the fun of the upcoming walk in the waves. And so she missed Frank's sharply indrawn breath and his open enjoyment of her modest strip.

Frank was entranced. How could he ever, he was asking himself, how could he ever have thought Bonanza Coombs was skinny?

Those long, lissome legs skinny? Those narrow hips, that tiny waist skinny? Those breasts, firm and high and just the right size for a man's eager palm, skinny?

Lest he disgrace himself—no secrets could be kept in the brief trunks he wore—Frank abruptly turned away and forced his attention onto the crowds beyond. In control again, he turned back to Bonnie. "Ready?"

He caught her staring at him with all the emotions he'd been feeling plain in her eyes for all the world—for him—to see.

Never in his life had Frank wanted something the way he wanted to make love to Bonanza Coombs right then and there. The desire he saw in her eyes, the admiration, the wonder—it was everything he'd been feeling, was feeling again. And more. To hell with the walk, he wanted to say. To hell with this picnic. Let's go home, Bonanza. Let's make love.

And if she hadn't been who she was, that's exactly what he would have said.

But this was Bonanza. This was Addie Filmore's granddaughter. And as if that weren't enough to make him proceed with delicacy and finesse, there still was the fact that this was a young woman who'd been

hurt. He wanted to heal her, not casually yank her into
bed and hurt her some more. He wanted—

Hell!

"Let's go take that walk." Grabbing Bonnie's hand,
Frank all but dragged her behind him as he stalked
across the beach toward the water.

He was mad at her. What had she done? For the life
of her Bonnie couldn't think of a thing. She'd stared
at him—who wouldn't have? He was gorgeous. Maybe
she'd made him uncomfortable, or maybe she'd made
him think she was—

Oh, my God, he wouldn't be thinking she was like
Loretta, would he?

"I was admiring your swimsuit," she said, trotting
to keep up with Frank's superbrisk pace. "Like, I
don't want you to think I was staring at *you* or anything."

At that he stopped and faced her. One look at her
anxious expression and he was hauling her against his
chest with a helpless, half-exasperated laugh. "Baby,
if that's supposed to make me feel better, it doesn't."
He gave her a squeeze, affectionate and nonthreaten-
ing. "You're something, Bonnie, you know that?"

Bonnie knew no such thing. But the way he said it,
with laughter and tenderness roughening his voice, she
could almost believe it. Laughing, she let him pull her
into the water. And she gasped.

If she'd thought the waters off Long Beach, California, were cold, stepping foot into the Pacific some
thousand miles north convinced her otherwise. Here
she feared her feet were about to turn into instant
clumps of ice.

"Yeow!" she yelped as the first breaker engulfed
her up to the knees, and then she did a dance that was

vividly reminiscent of a movie cowboy dodging bullets aimed at his feet as she tried to keep her own out of the water. She raced up the shore, calling back to Frank, "How can you stand it?"

"I'm a *man*," he called, and with a Tarzan yell, pounded his chest.

The sight of Bonnie laughing aloud without restraint, her head thrown back and the slender, graceful curve of her neck exposed to the sun made Frank feel ten feet tall. She was having a good time, and he was giving it to her.

He vowed that nothing would mar this day.

Their walk was fun. Bonnie found sand dollars, which she'd never known before. She watched and listened, fascinated, as Frank broke one open and told her the legend about the marks on them.

"They're lovely."

"What, the story or the shell?"

"Both." Bonnie's smile got tangled with his. Something was stealing her breath. "Don't you think?" she asked, her voice thin and shaky.

Frank thought *she* was lovely, and he let his eyes tell her so. Noting her blush, he tried for conversation.

"So are you Catholic?" he asked, surprising himself.

"Gosh." She straightened from the crouch she'd been in while listening to the legend. "I don't know. I don't think so. I was never anything until I went to church with Ellie. She was Methodist. Is it important?"

"No. I just wondered." Just then nothing was important besides keeping Bonnie happy and smiling. He'd wanted to find out something personal about her, was all. "I'm hungry," he said. "How about you?"

"Starved."

They broke out the lunch: cold, breaded pork chops, potato salad, fruit and mineral water.

"I made this," Bonnie said.

It was delicious. "The water, too?"

She swatted him. "You're always teasing."

"Oh, no." Frank allowed some of his pent-up feelings to show. "Not always."

Blushing, Bonnie swatted him again.

After lunch, replete, they laid back and rested. But Frank was too aware of Bonnie's scantily clad form stretched out beside him, of her arm touching his now and then, of their thighs a mere breath apart to just lie there.

Restless, he sat up and scanned the beach. Except for some kids frolicking in the surf, it seemed to be fiesta time all around. He glanced at Bonnie, still flat on her back, eyes closed. Taking his time, he let his eyes travel the length of her, follow each peak and valley, each dip and curve. And felt himself getting hot all over again.

Damn.

He reached into the backpack he'd brought, pulled out a dog-eared paperback, found his place and commenced to read.

"What're you reading?"

Frank had just gotten engrossed. "Hmm?"

"I said what're you reading?"

"Michener." He showed her the book. "Have you read it?"

Suddenly Bonnie wished she'd kept her mouth shut. "Umm, no. No, I haven't."

"But you've read his others surely. Seems like everybody's read him. What about *Tales of The South Pacific?*"

"I . . . umm . . . I think I saw the movie. . . ." A cold sweat was breaking out all over Bonnie's body. She'd just bet he thought her ignorant. "On video. Ellie liked to rent the classics. . . ."

She just *knew* he thought her ignorant, he was looking at her so funny. "I really liked it," she hurried to add. "Have you seen it?"

"Yeah, I have." Why was Bonnie so jittery? Hell, he'd almost call it panicky. She didn't read Michener, so what? A lot of people couldn't stand the guy's stuff. Besides, he belatedly recalled with chagrin, it wasn't as if she'd grown up in an environment conducive to long, lazy hours of serious reading.

Frank tried to discharge some of the tension he sensed was building between them. "Every now and then I get in the mood for this stuff—" He slightly raised the book he held in his hand, using his index finger as a bookmark. "But by and large I'm a mystery junkie. Dashiell Hammett, J. A. Janz . . ."

Bonnie's expression grew steadily more shuttered.

"Agatha Christie?" He laughed, forcing it, and again changed direction. "Hey, I've even read a romance or two. Mom and Marie eat those up." He whistled through his teeth and wiggled his eyebrows. "Pret-ty steamy stuff."

Bonnie didn't react to his attempted humor. Nor did she speak. She was sitting up now and staring at the ocean, her mouth in a thin, downturned line.

"Which isn't to say that they weren't well written," Frank added, studying her profile with a frown of his own. Dammit, what was getting Bonanza so steamed?

Frank could see the harmony of the day disintegrate without having a clue as to why and with no idea how to salvage it.

Figuring he had nothing to lose, he tossed his book down and taking hold of Bonnie's shoulders, turned her to face him. "All right," he said. "What happened? What'd I say?"

"Nothing." She wouldn't meet his eyes.

"Don't give me that." He gave her a light shake. "Talk to me, Bonanza."

Silence.

He gripped her chin. "Will you look at me? Please?" he added softly when still she balked. "Tell me what's wrong, Bonnie. It can't be about reading Michener, so come on, tell me."

She didn't answer, but the eyes she reluctantly lifted to his were dark with something that reminded him of a deer he'd once unintentionally cornered. Fear. There was fear in her eyes, and a most unsettling expression of resignation.

Frank intuitively surmised that whatever it was he'd said or done, he'd inadvertently put Bonnie in a position from which she could see no dignified escape, no out. And so she'd resigned herself to accepting the consequences.

The tip of her tongue came out to moisten her lips, and she parted them to speak.

But suddenly Frank didn't want to hear what she'd say. Suddenly, he had the most awful feeling that if he didn't stop her from making yet another confession, not only the day, but their budding relationship would be irreparably ruined.

He didn't want either of those things to happen. He wanted this day to be as perfect as it was possible to be, given the present unpleasantness, and he wanted even more to let a relationship between them ripen and mature into something . . . more. When that had happened—and he was sure now, he wanted that more than anything—there would be time enough for coming to terms with such minor problems as differing tastes in reading materials. Hell, he wouldn't care if she read nothing but the Sunday comics, the way his pop did. Or even if she didn't read at all, for crissake.

He didn't care about any of that, but it was obvious Bonnie did. So much so that to talk about it would really cost her. Cost her too much.

Frank did the only thing he could think of to keep Bonnie from speaking. He kissed her.

And Bonnie was too stunned to do more than just sit there and let him.

It wasn't a kiss of passion. It wasn't a long kiss or a soft kiss. It was a kiss of purpose, hard and short. And oh, so timely.

It was over before Bonnie could gather her scattered wits, and it took a moment for her to react when Frank leapt to his feet and began to run.

"Last one in is a rotten fish," he called over his shoulder as he raced toward the water.

Too weak with relief at the reprieve she'd been granted to give it her best, and too happy to care about how frigid the water was, Bonnie took off after him.

They didn't get into anything heavy the rest of the day. They enjoyed the moment, each other's company and the nebulous but steadily growing anticipation of something wonderful awaiting them at the end of the day. When it came time to head for home, Bonnie shed her still damp bathing suit and, not having thought to bring underwear, simply put on her loose-fitting shorts and T-shirt.

She sat close to Frank on the ride home. He'd patted the spot next to him as she'd gotten into the car, and Bonnie hadn't quibbled. It had grown chilly, the way summer days and evenings were prone to do without warning in the Pacific Northwest. Neither Frank nor Bonnie had brought anything warm to put on. Sitting closely side by side warmed each of them.

They walked up the walk to the house together, too. Not holding hands or touching—they were each carrying the day's paraphernalia—but close, nevertheless. They didn't speak—there seemed nothing left to say—but they were excruciatingly aware of each other. And of the fact that in just a few short moments, they'd be inside the house. Alone.

They climbed the porch steps, and Bonnie hugged the blanket and towels she carried to her chest as Frank unlocked the door. He pushed it open, then waited for Bonnie to precede him into the foyer. He pushed the door shut with his foot and kept his eyes on the gentle sway of her slender hips as he followed her into the kitchen.

Not a word was said.

Frank set the picnic cooler on the counter next to the sink; Bonnie tossed the blanket and towels into the washing machine in the corner. She left the lid up and didn't start the machine. She just stood there, staring at the agitator, trying to decide.

But when she turned and saw Frank, she knew she'd decided long ago. That morning, probably. Or maybe even the night when he'd tucked her into bed like a helpless infant, maybe she'd decided then to show him that she wasn't a child, but a woman. His woman, if he wanted her to be.

Across the room, by the sink, Frank was leaning against the edge of the counter, watching her. When she turned and lifted her eyes to his, he took his time reading the message in her gaze, all the while sending back a steady, potent one of his own.

He wanted to be sure she knew. He needed to be sure she was willing. And he wanted to leave her no doubts as to what he intended to do.

Bonnie had no doubts. And no reservations. She stayed where she was and kept her eyes locked on Frank's as he pushed away from the counter and walked toward her. Her breath caught in a rush of anticipation. A funny sort of shudder rippled across her body, leaving delicious eddies of sensation in its wake. Even before Frank touched her, even before he closed the small remaining gap between their bodies, she felt him, smelled him, wanted him.

And it was she who closed the gap.

With a tiny, ragged cry of longing, she took his face in both her hands, raised on tiptoe and laid her mouth on his. It was the first kiss she had ever initiated, but then, Frank was the first man, the only man, she had ever wanted. The only man she'd ever wanted to kiss, wanted to have, wanted to hold.

Frank Malloy was the only man she had ever wanted to... *love*.

She let her hands relax, let them soften on Frank's face. She smoothed them gently along his jaw, exploring the slight roughness of his five o'clock shadow, tugging on earlobes that were as soft as velvet between thumb and forefinger of each hand. Gently she circled a finger along the whorl of each ear, then tenderly probed.

And all the while her lips nibbled on his like on some costly, delicate pastry, with her tongue emerging now and then to lick and feather, as if to catch a wayward crumb.

As was her way when learning or trying anything new, Bonnie concentrated completely on what she was doing. All her attention was centered on Frank; all her efforts were geared toward showing him and making him feel the tingling heat and desperate longings that were turning her own insides to swirling water.

She couldn't know how successful she was.

Frank had never been as thoroughly seduced as Bonanza was seducing him right there in her kitchen. With just the touch of her lips and the play of her fingers, she was reducing him to a mass of white-hot, quivering desire. She had yet to part his lips, had yet to move beyond the barrier of his teeth into the expectant heat of his mouth. She had yet to touch her tongue to his. Her fingers had yet to become urgent, had yet to tunnel into his hair, grip his head and hold it still for her kiss. Her passion had still to be aroused.

Until it did, however, her tenderness was bringing him to his knees.

They'd gone weak in a way they hadn't since the first time he'd been with a girl. His hands, slowly moving down the long, sleek curve of her back, were trembling. His lips beneath hers were parted and eager.

He couldn't take any more.

With a groan, a rumbling growl of primal need, Frank became the aggressor. He hardened his lips. Catching Bonnie's with unerring intention, he put an end to nibbling exploration and set a course toward complete possession.

His hands, too, though trembling still, had reached their goal. They cupped the sweet mounds of Bonnie's derriere and pulled her against him, lifting and fitting until she was riding the thigh he had pushed between hers. Deepening the kiss, his tongue pursuing and capturing Bonnie's, he became the seducer and she the seduced.

No remnant horror rose up to mar the magic of this moment for Bonnie. She knew nothing, remembered nothing, wanted nothing but the here, the now. Frank's touch, Frank's kiss. Frank's body tightly pressed to hers. Frank's lips slanting and probing and stirring up her senses more deeply than anything ever had. She never wanted the moment to end, never wanted to let him go.

With everything she had, with *more* than she could ever have imagined she had, Bonnie responded to Frank's every touch and caress. Where he went, she followed. Where his hand touched, so hers touched, too. And when he tugged free her T-shirt and his hand slid across naked skin, she shivered with anticipation and again followed suit.

Muscles, smooth and hard. She stroked them, felt them, clutched them as Frank was clutching her in a sudden spasm of passion and need. His hands slid around to the front, his open palm brushed across the hardened bud of her nipple, and, as Bonnie's found its masculine counterpart in its nest of hair, Frank's hips bucked hard against hers.

His thigh moved, he pressed her closer. Flames like those of a wildfire shot up the core of her straight to her heart. Her arms wrapped around him; she clung to him, tight. He was her rock in a tempest so wild and glorious, it threatened to sweep her senses completely.

Feeling Bonnie's total surrender, Frank swung her up into his arms and headed for the bedroom.

Chapter Nine

Frank carried Bonnie to the old-fashioned four-poster without once lifting his mouth from hers. Laying her across the bed and following her down onto it was one smooth movement. With her arms still circling his neck, his arms clasping her back and her legs wrapped around his middle, they were entwined like a knot in a rope. Their mouths slanted and twisted until their lips were fused. Their tongues delved deeply, playing a game of touch and retreat and establishing the rhythm for things to come.

Their hands feverishly delved beneath the few items of clothing each wore, then impatiently tugged and pulled until they wore nothing. Heat-slickened bodies touched and rubbed, giving birth to a host of new and exciting sensations that drove the passion they shared into frenzy.

"Bonnie," Frank rasped, panting. "Lord, girl, you're—you're killing me." His lips nibbled and nipped at the delicate bone of her jaw, the corners of her mouth, her chin, while his hand stroked the concavity of her stomach with slow, circular motions, creating a tempest of want in the pit of it.

Bonnie writhed on the bed in response to Frank's tormenting touches. Her hips rose and fell in response to the urgent thrust of his. She clung to him, kissed him, touched him.

His groan was ragged with desperation. "I want you, Bonnie. Oh, sweet, sweet girl, I want you so much. So badly..."

Bonnie responded to his need without thinking. "Oh, Frank," she murmured, "Frank. I love you. I love you."

"Be mine," Frank whispered against her lips. "Let me have you, baby." His hand moved lower. "Let me, sweetheart. I need you."

"Yes." The words were a mere feather stroke against his ear, an exhalation.

But he'd heard. His caresses grew bolder.

Bonnie's breath caught. Again she gasped his name.

"It's all right," Frank assured her. "It's all right."

"Oh, please..." Helplessly, as waves of pleasure carried her out of herself, Bonnie writhed beneath his touch. She shuddered.

"Yes," Frank murmured, his lips touching her face in a series of openmouthed kisses. "Yes, yes..." He kissed her eyes, her brow, her ear. His tongue explored the shell of it, teased and tantalized and stroked just the way his nimble fingers were doing elsewhere.

"You're so sweet, so hot. Ah, Bonnie..." Frank knew he couldn't wait any longer to make her his completely. "Say you want me, love. I need to hear it, baby."

"I want you." Bonnie gasped the words as spasms of pleasure rippled through her. "Oh, Frank, I want... I want..."

"I know.... I know...." Carefully, Frank moved over her. They were belly to belly. "Are you protected, Bon?" he gasped out before relinquishing reason and rational thought and giving in to pure mindless passion.

"Hmm?" Bonnie urged his lips back to hers, not wanting to talk now, only wanting fulfillment of the promise his kisses, his body and his hands had made.

"Are you on something?" Frank had to force himself to care. He was bursting, hurting.... "I don't have anything with me, love," he said between labored breaths, "or I'd take care of it...."

"What?" Bonnie was reluctant to surface from the sea of desire in which she'd been submerged, but some of the urgency in Frank's voice filtered through. She blinked, tried to focus on the ruggedly handsome, beloved face only inches away.

His eyes were bright sapphires in a face contorted by something bordering on pain. And what he'd asked her sank in. Was she protected?

"Oh, Frank." A world of regret was in her voice. She touched his cheek. "I'm sorry."

A moan of pure pain and disappointment shuddered through Frank's now clenched teeth. His head fell forward until his brow rested against Bonnie's as he struggled for control over his clamoring senses.

"But," he ground out, frustration prodding him, "how the hell . . . ?"

"I've never had to be before."

And she shouldn't have to be this time, either, Frank grimly conceded. It should've been his responsibility. But, damn it all—

"A bit careless, don't you think, always relying on your partner?"

Where had the magic gone? Bonnie felt tears well up. She furiously swallowed them. "Dammit, there has been no other partner."

Frank couldn't help it, the notion that he'd been seduced by a virgin was too ridiculous. He laughed.

And found himself flat on his back with Bonnie above him like the wrath of Hades. Never had she felt so hurt and humiliated. To think she'd been ready to love and trust him. "You bastard," she snarled, shaking all over. "Get out."

And then, to her everlasting mortification, she burst into tears.

Frank wouldn't have felt more sick to his stomach if she'd punched him in it. "Bonanza, listen. . . ."

"No." She turned and fled into the bathroom. Frank was right behind her, but the door slammed in his face. The click of the lock followed.

His open palm hit the door. He hung his head. "Bonnie, don't do this. Talk to me, hit me. Anything. I'm sorry. I didn't mean to laugh. It was just so incredible, so unbelievable. . . ."

"Considering who I am, is that it?"

"No! Yes." God, but he'd been a jerk! Furious with himself, Frank's fist hit the door. "Can you blame me? For Pete's sake, Bonanza, there're sixteen-year-olds in convents who'll never be virgins again. You're twenty-one...."

"And from the streets."

"Yeah." Frank nodded and sighed. He'd blown it. Instead of loving Bonanza, he'd hurt her. Instead of instilling confidence in her, he'd proved what she'd always maintained: men, especially cops, were bastards. He stepped back.

The door opened. Bonnie stood wrapped in a towel, pale but dry-eyed. "It's no good, is it?" she said.

"I don't know." Frank looked down at his feet. They were bare, as he was naked. He raised his eyes to Bonnie's and caught the longing with which she was looking at him. "Bonnie." He took a step forward.

She retreated. "Don't, Frank, please. I'd like you to go now."

Grimly, he nodded. Palms forward, he backed away from her. "This isn't over, Bonnie," he said. "You know that, don't you?"

Bonnie closed the bathroom door and let her head drop against it. No, it wasn't over, she knew that. How could it be when it had never begun?

For the next several days, Frank made it a point to make himself scarce. His day with Bonanza at the beach and, more to the point, its first passionate, then disastrous conclusion needed thinking about. He had to clarify to himself what his feelings for Bonanza Coombs were, and he needed to come to terms with them. And afterward he'd take whatever action was indicated.

The things he'd learned about her put an entirely new light on things. She wasn't who and what he'd taken for granted she was. She wasn't experienced. She hadn't "been around" in the sexual sense. In spite of the abuse she'd suffered at the hands of that creep, she'd remained miraculously untouched.

At this stage of his life, there was no way Frank was going to change that state of affairs without serious thought to the consequences. Bad enough that other members of his profession had done Bonanza dirt, he wasn't going to heap more of it on her if he could help it.

And so he stayed away from his apartment. He didn't bunk at his folks', either, since Bonnie was liable to show up there to spend time with Jennifer or to visit with his parents, who had extended her a carte-blanche invitation. Funny how they'd taken to her, especially his mother, who, with people in general and out of towners in particular, tended to bide her time.

He'd bedded down at Saint Christopher's on many occasions in the past—like when things got sticky at home in his younger days or when Addie had had painters in. Or at those times when he'd been too exhausted to drive all the way home after doing double shifts as well as volunteering.

There was a lumpy sofa in the cubbyhole that served as the athletic director's office, and that's where he slept.

Bonnie told herself she didn't miss him. She was too busy helping Jimmy Thurston with the paint job on her house to even notice Frank never came home. Or so she told herself. She also told herself she'd just as soon he never came home, but, somehow, she didn't believe it.

Jennifer hadn't seen him, either, but she said Uncle Frankie sometimes had to work out of town. Bonnie, though ashamed of herself for pumping the little girl in the course of their first art lesson, took some comfort from that.

After Frank left her part of the house that Sunday night, the ceiling had creaked beneath his tread for quite some time, telling her he was restless and pacing. Bonnie felt better knowing she wasn't the only one upset.

Just before dawn she'd heard his step on the stairs, followed by the click of the lock as the front door shut behind him. He'd left.

Bonnie had gotten up then. And she hadn't slept very much in the five days since.

She could feel the resultant fatigue in her bones as she and Jennifer walked hand in hand across the shaded grounds of Saint Christopher's Mission on Friday afternoon. Bonnie had persuaded Marie to let Jennifer be part of the class she taught at the mission in addition to the two private sessions a week they'd agreed on.

Drawing pictures had always been a wonderful outlet for Bonnie. For as far back as she could remember, she'd been able to pour all of her troubles and woes into the pictures she drew, even when a stub of a pencil and the inside of a torn-open cereal box were the only things she had to work with.

At the day care, too, Bonnie had noticed that children who had trouble articulating or who, perhaps, had no one at home who took the time to listen to them, would draw pictures of those things that were on their minds.

After hearing that Jennifer's stutter had started with her father's death, Bonnie's thoughts had begun to churn. After her visit to the child's room, where she had observed how the stutter lessened when Jennifer held her father's picture and talked of him, an idea had blossomed. She'd presented it to Marie the next day, and so Jennifer's private drawing lessons had begun. Marie had wanted to pay something for them, but Bonnie had quite adamantly refused. She planned to become a preschool or special ed teacher one day, she'd told Marie. She regarded teaching Jennifer like training of sorts for that.

Bonnie and Jennifer spent two hours—Tuesday and Thursday afternoons were the agreed-upon days— talking and drawing and just being together, all of which seemed to ease the anxiety and tension Bonnie sensed in the child. The first day they'd drawn—or tried to draw smiles. All kinds of them, each other's and anybody else's they could come up with, and Bonnie had confided that she, too, had inherited her father's smile. She'd delighted the child by dragging out one of Addie's photographs of Roy Rogers Filmore to prove it.

The second session, they'd worked on drawing their father's faces while telling each other stories about some particularly good times they'd spent with their dads. Bonnie freely used her imagination to enlarge on the limited encounters she'd had with her father and made up several hilarious ones out of thin air.

As Jennifer recounted sleigh rides and Halloween and summertime picnics, she hardly stuttered at all.

She was skipping along at Bonnie's side now, jerking Bonnie's hand with each hop and skip as they crossed the cool expanse of Saint C's lawn, still fragrant from Jimmy Thurston's last mowing.

"L-look, B-Bonnie," she exclaimed suddenly, pointing. "There's, there's Uncle Frankie's c-car."

Bonnie had already seen it. And her heart had leapt into her throat.

"C-can we go f-find him, Bonnie, p-please?"

"Maybe after the class, Jen, okay?" Maybe he'd be gone by then. Meanwhile, please God, let him stay wherever it was he was. "Everybody's waiting for us already."

"Oh. Okay." Jennifer's tone left no doubt that just then art class had been relegated to second position on her list of priorities. Though she walked along without further complaint, she no longer skipped.

Once inside the classroom, however, she was soon as absorbed in her project as everyone else. Bonnie had seated the little girl next to the gap-toothed Lester Jackson, who was delighted to have someone new to impress with his countless airplane renderings. Jennifer, tongue sticking out of the corner of her mouth in concentration, was now drawing airplanes, too.

Bonnie stood at one of the three easels set up near the large window in back of the room, helping a very pregnant young woman with her brush strokes. Old Max, one of the homeless who'd found shelter at Saint C's, was painting at another easel. It was something grand in bold reds and blues that only he could recognize, but which Bonnie praised nonetheless. The class wasn't about precision and mastering of a craft so much as it was about interaction and expressing of whatever lay inside.

Anger seemed to have, for too long, lain dormant inside of Margaret Sloan. The battered wife of an alcoholic, she'd finally had the courage to leave the man only last week. She suddenly startled the entire class by letting loose a bloodcurdling scream and smashing her fists into the canvas on the third easel.

Bonnie rushed over to her, reassuring her thunderstruck students. "Don't worry. Everything's fine.

"Margaret," she said gently to the now quietly weeping woman, putting an arm around her waist as she spoke. "Here, let me—"

Let me help you, she'd intended to say, but before she could finish the sentence, Margaret reared back with another feral scream, swung and backhanded Bonnie neatly across the face.

The force of the blow had Bonnie tripping backward into a rickety, three-legged coat tree, taking it with her as she sprawled on the floor. The back of her head connected smartly with the classroom wall. Jennifer's high-pitched, "Bonnie!" was the last thing Bonanza heard.

Two heads and two pairs of sapphire blue eyes—one pair shimmering with tears, the other darkened with worry—were mere inches from her face when Bonnie came to. They swam in and out of focus for a few dizzying moments, and she blinked to clear her vision.

"Wha' happen'?" she mumbled. "F-Frank? Jen . . . ?"

"None other," came the gruff reply, and one pair of the blue eyes became shadowed by a frown. "How're you feeling?"

"Ouch," Bonnie said, trying for humor because, with her faculties gradually returning to something like normal, she noted the panic and lack of color on Jennifer's face.

She tasted blood inside her mouth and carefully probed with her tongue. Her teeth seemed intact, but her tongue smarted. She'd probably bitten it somewhere along the way. She tried for a smile. "But I'll live."

"You're going to have a shiner." Frank arranged her head more comfortably in his lap.

"Gee, swell."

"And there's a knot at the back of your head the size of a baseball."

"Terrific." Bonnie tossed Jennifer a glance without moving her head. It pounded whenever she did. "You ever had one o' those?"

Jennifer mutely shook her head, but, Bonnie noted with satisfaction, her cheeks had color again and the panic no longer lurked in her eyes.

"Well, don't bother trying for one," Bonnie told her. "The experience isn't all it's cracked up to be."

"I'm taking you to the doctor," Frank said. He figured his knees wouldn't wobble if he stood up now. Hearing the commotion in Bonnie's classroom and then Jennifer's terrified scream, he'd barreled into the room at a dead run. Seeing Bonnie in an unconscious heap on the floor had made his heart stop. He'd fallen to his knees and slid to her side like a runner making first base. His hands shaking like aspen leaves, he'd gathered her onto his lap. "It's possible you've got a concussion."

"I don't." Bonnie didn't want the doctor. She had no insurance, didn't have nearly enough money on her to pay him in cash. Writing out a check was still a bit tricky for her, too. "I'm fine," she maintained. "Please, no doctor."

"You're in no shape to determine how you are, all right?" Frank scooped her into his arms and smoothly got to his feet. "Come on, Jen. Get Bonnie's purse and let's go."

"I've got a class to teach," Bonnie protested. "Set me down."

Frank kept right on going. "Class is out for the day."

"Wait." They were in the wide, vaulted, marble-floored hall and heading for the exit. "What about Margaret? I want to tell her not to worry—"

"Father Joe's with her." Frank's tone softened, as did his expression. "Nothing's going to happen to her, Bon."

"It wasn't her fault. She's been through so much...."

"I know. And she's in good hands here." His arms briefly tightened, bringing Bonnie close to his chest. "Just as you are."

"Please, Frank—" Bonnie tried pleading. "No doctor."

"Why not?"

"For one thing, I don't need one. For another, I don't have one."

"I do."

"But I don't have any money," she wailed.

"I do." They were at his car. He gently set her down on the passenger seat. Jennifer scrambled into the back. She was being awfully quiet.

Bonnie gingerly turned her head to look at her. "You okay, Jen?"

Tears suddenly filled the child's eyes again. As she nodded, they spilled down her cheeks. "I..." Her lips quivered around a sob. "I thought you were—you were..."

"Oh, baby." Awkwardly, her head pounding, Bonnie twisted around and touched the girl's crumpled face. "I'm fine. Really."

"I was so scared."

Frank, sliding in behind the steering wheel, heard what his niece was saying. He, too, turned to face the back seat. "Hey," he said softly, "that's okay. I was pretty scared, myself."

"B-but, but you're not *cry*-ing," Jennifer wailed.

"That's what you think." Frank's gaze slid to Bonnie's. His eyes were dark, somber. "Inside of me I am."

They had dropped off Jennifer and the doctor had confirmed Bonnie's self-diagnosis: no concussion, just a nasty lump, a throbbing headache and a black eye. He'd fed Bonnie a couple of pain pills, handed Frank a small sample packet of mild sedatives to give Bonnie at home and told Bonnie to rest up the next day or two.

"See," Bonnie groused as they drove home. "A complete waste of twenty-five dollars."

"Best money I ever spent," Frank said. Now that he knew Bonnie was all right, he was happy to give her an argument.

"I'm paying you back as soon as we get to the house."

"You'll do nothing but get in bed, young lady. In fact, I'm putting you there myself, just to be sure."

Bonnie's headache was waning, leaving her head clear enough for her thoughts to be diverted to the last time Frank Malloy had been in her bedroom. She really didn't want a repeat. So she said, "No, you're not."

Frank leisurely turned the car into Maple Street. He shot her a glance. "Wanna bet?"

"No." Their gazes briefly tangled. Blood surged to Bonnie's heart, and she swallowed. "I really don't think your coming into my bedroom again is a good idea, Frank."

"Think lust will overcome me?" he teased, hoping to ease the tension he felt building between them.

Bonnie blushed and looked away.

Tenderness made Frank's throat ache. He caught her hand and brought it to his lips. His eyes were on the road as he gently chewed on one of her knuckles, then kissed it.

"I'm just a dumb cop, but I've realized something these past few days. You're special, Bonnie," he told her with a warm and very serious sideways glance. "And I assure you my plans for you don't include a quick toss in the hay. All right?"

So what *did* they include? Bonnie felt a stab of pain that had nothing to do with her head. She wished she knew how Frank felt about her, but there was no way she could ask. In truth, she was afraid of what he might say if she did.

What if he told her he had no plans for her at all in his life? No room? There she'd be, alone again....

She tried to return Frank's warm smile and blamed the trouble she was having with it on her injuries.

"So don't worry," he was saying. "All right? We'll talk about it very soon." He laid her hand in her lap. "For now, however, I'll just put you to bed, give you your medicine and split."

He was as good as his word. With all the dispatch and impersonal solicitude of a professional nurse, he had Bonnie out of her dress and sandals and in bed with an ice pack on her forehead. He made her swallow the pills, then tucked the sheet and blanket up under her chin and darkened the room.

Halfway out the door, he stopped to look back at her. "I'll be upstairs if you need me. Now sleep."

When Bonnie awoke to dimly lit darkness several hours later, however, Frank was not upstairs but right there, sitting beside her bed.

Funny, she thought, dreamily drinking in the sight of him. Funny, how that didn't startle her. How it didn't alarm her.

Frank was thinking how lovely she looked. Deliciously sleepy, a little fuzzy around the edges from the sedative, Bonanza was beautiful to him in spite of the shiner that was puffing her cheek and spreading like a splash of greenish purple paint into her left eye.

For long moments neither spoke as they looked at each other.

"Hi," Frank finally said, his voice rusty.

"Hi." Bonnie didn't return the tentative smile he was giving her.

Frank cleared his throat, a little uncomfortable, wondering if she thought he'd come down to spy on her. Or worse.

"I thought I heard you call," he said, which wasn't entirely true. He'd heard a thump, and thinking she might have fallen out of bed and hurt herself, he'd rushed downstairs.

Sam had almost tripped him up as he shot out of Bonnie's studio room into the hall. Frank had known then that the noise he'd heard had been the cat jumping through the open window that had become his access of choice into Bonnie's domain. With Bonnie now faithfully taking her antihistamines, Sam knew he was a welcome caller.

Tonight Frank had unceremoniously booted him upstairs, however. After which he'd decided to check on Bonnie, just in case, and had somehow gotten stuck on the chair....

"What time is it?" Bonnie became aware that her headache was gone but that it had left wads of cotton in its wake. It filled her head with a fuzzy warmth that now languidly spread through the rest of her, too.

"Just after midnight."

Frank told himself he ought to be going, but made no move to do so.

"You hungry? Can I fix you something?"

Bonnie slowly shook her head. She was happy just to lie there and look at him. He was so handsome, so nice. How could she have ever thought otherwise? How could she have ever wanted him gone? Now...

Tears of self-pity, easily tapped in her presently hurt and befuddled condition, rushed to her eyes. What would she ever do without him? He was everything Ellie had been—a friend. Such a good friend. Except Frank was more, too.

Frank was her love.

She wondered what she could do to make him love her in return and, knowing she had nothing to offer, closed her eyes on a wave of despair. Tears spilled down her cheeks.

Bonnie was crying. The instant he saw, Frank was off the chair and bending over her. "Bonnie! What is it, hon—are you in pain?" He touched her brow. "Is it your head? Your face? What?"

Bonnie turned her face to the wall. "N-no."

"What, then?" He gently urged her head back toward him. "Tell me, Bon."

She looked into his eyes, searching for something more, something deeper than the caring and concern she saw there. She wanted to see again the heat, the desire he'd shown her on Sunday. She shifted her gaze to his lips, let it linger, then looked back up into his eyes.

Frank got the message with a jolt. Bonanza wanted him to kiss her. He almost groaned aloud. Lord knew he'd been sitting here wanting to kiss her—and more— for the past several hours. And he'd called himself an animal for having such feelings when she was laid low.

Frank had done a lot of thinking during the past five days, and he'd reached some conclusions. One of them was that he owed it to Bonnie to let *her* make the next move. If she wanted whatever was happening between them to escalate into a full-fledged love affair, then she had to be the one to initiate the first step. After all, she had more to lose than he had.

She'd told him she loved him—oh, yes, he'd heard. But he better than anyone knew people said things in the heat of passion, when they were hungry, needy.... Before either one of them got that hungry and needy again, some things had to be said with a cool head.

But not now. Not when Bonanza was half out of it from the sedative; not when she was flat on her back and vulnerable; not when she wasn't thinking straight.

He kissed the tip of her nose and immediately drew back. "You need to sleep," he said gruffly. "And so do I. Alone," he added when she opened her mouth to speak. He didn't need her to say the words; he could see the invitation in her eyes. "How about we have dinner together somewhere—"

"I could cook us something."

"No. We'll eat and talk somewhere public." He let his gaze send a message now, too. The flicker of her lashes and the way her tongue emerged to lick her lips told him it had been received. "From here on in, I want everything between us out in the open and understood, Bonanza," he went on huskily. "And then *you* take it from there." Their eyes clung as he slowly drew back. "Understood?"

Choked by a million emotions, Bonnie could only nod.

"All right." Frank was standing next to the bed. "Now I'm scheduled to work some pretty hairy shifts for the next few days. How about Thursday?"

"I'm sorry, I can't."

"I know you've usually got somewhere to go that night," Frank said, "but couldn't you change it this once?"

Bonnie's face paled. "No. I'm sorry." She said it flatly. Her reading lessons were inviolate. "No, I can't."

Frank wanted to ask why not, but Bonnie's expression, so animated only moments before, had now grown still and shuttered. He searched her eyes for a clue, but they, though steady on his, gave nothing away.

"Okay." He forced a careless shrug. "Don't worry about it." He walked to the door, calling himself an idiot for being bothered by Bonnie's flat refusal, but he was bugged by it just the same. Nor did it help to tell himself that she was her own woman, that she had a right to her secrets.

He turned to look back at her, frowning, and caught her staring at him with despair and pleading in her eyes. "Don't be mad at me, Frank," she said.

"I'm not."

"I'm free any other day...."

The hopeful inflection at the end of her statement made him feel like a heel. He twisted his lips into a self-deprecating grin. "I'll see you Friday, then."

Chapter Ten

The question of where Bonanza spent her Thursday evenings—and with whom—kept nagging at Frank. It would crop up at odd hours and in the oddest situations, like at eleven-thirty in the morning while he was testifying in court. Or while brushing his teeth moments before falling into bed at the end of a long shift. Or while picking himself up off the ground after the drunk and disorderly he was taking in Tuesday night decked him.

Each time he cursed himself, told himself it was none of his business—and then went on to make a mental list of all the places she could be going: to the movies; to the library; to a class in basket weaving. She could be baby-sitting, visiting friends he didn't know she had. Or she could be engaged in any other of a hundred activities the nature of which he had no idea.

Yet she could have skipped all of those if she'd wanted to.

He knew, without being vain, that she really did want to have that dinner with him. She wanted to talk with him. She wanted to come to an understanding as much as he did. He knew this. It'd been as plain as day in her actions, her expressions, her words. Except not on Thursday.

Which meant she had a fixed, unchangeable appointment. And that, to Frank, indicated there had to be another person involved. A person whose time was inflexible. A person who was so important to her, she wouldn't even consider not seeing him one week, or possibly inconveniencing him.

Him?

It stood to reason it was a him, Frank thought in response to the niggling question. It had been his experience that women didn't hesitate to break assignations with other women, as a rule.

Besides, he reasoned, pulling the car to the curb about half a block from the house he and Bonanza occupied, Bonnie had exhibited the kind of behavior—defensive evasiveness bordering on hostility—that he'd observed in people in trouble, people with something to hide, more times than he could count.

Something was going on on Thursday nights that Bonanza Coombs did not want him to know about.

The moment he'd come to that conclusion, he decided to find out what that something was.

Checking his watch, Frank slid down in the seat of his car till he sat on his tailbone. Tired—he'd worked graveyard the past two nights and hadn't gotten all that much sleep today—he relaxed his head against the corner where the seat met the door.

Bonnie wouldn't be out for another fifteen minutes or so, he figured. Marie and Jennifer had left only a few minutes before he'd gone downstairs to drive his car around the block. He'd heard the shower on his way out.

Bonnie was getting herself all spruced up and ready. Frank set his jaw. Tonight, by damn, he'd see for what or for whom. And maybe then, when they had their dinner and talk tomorrow, they'd have something else to discuss. . . .

There she came. Frank straightened and took the car out of Park without taking his eyes off Bonnie.

She was a sight in a pink summer dress that was fitted on top and had the kind of full, swirly skirt Frank loved to see on a woman. Especially one whose waist he could almost span with his two hands and whose legs were as long and shapely as Bonnie's were.

Keeping his foot on the break, Frank watched Bonnie stop on the porch steps and frown up at the gathering clouds in the sky.

"Yeah," he muttered. "Get an umbrella."

As if she'd heard him, she went back in, emerging again in minutes with a backpack slung over one shoulder. Not seeing an umbrella, Frank scowled, then shrugged. Maybe she'd stuck the damn thing into the backpack.

It was both pleasure and torture following Bonanza in the car at a discreet distance, watching the sassy swing and sway of hips and skirt as she walked briskly toward Denman's Café on Main Street. It doubled as the bus depot.

She should wear dresses more often, Frank reflected appreciatively. They very much underscored her femininity.

Suddenly he couldn't wait until tomorrow. To hell with this, he thought impatiently. What're you doing, sneaking after her like a schoolboy, Malloy? Get your tail in gear and step on it. Offer the lady a lift to wherever she's going. Talk on the way, and afterward, kiss her till you're both senseless and silly.

The notion appealed. He accelerated just as Bonnie began to run. What the hell?

The bus was pulling out of Denman's lot. Bonnie ran harder, waving with one hand, clutching the backpack with the other. The driver saw her and acknowledged her with a salute and a grin.

Frank slowed the car and eased it over to the curb, idling there as Bonnie boarded the waiting bus. The destination sign above the windshield read Olympia.

Maybe she had relatives there. Frank matched his speed to that of the bus and stayed two car lengths behind. Or maybe a girlhood friend.

Yeah, right, Malloy—just like you have friends and relatives in Outer Mongolia.

To distract himself, he turned on the radio. Loud. Then immediately muted it as a newscaster's voice almost deafened him. He switched to FM, found some rock and cranked the sound up again. That was better, he decided grimly. Not a man alive could think with this kind of racket assaulting his ears.

Bonnie got off the bus at the edge of town in an older, predominantly residential neighborhood. As the darkening skies had earlier promised, a drizzling rain had begun to fall. Ducking her head, Bonnie sprinted across the street so unexpectedly, Frank had to slam on the brakes to keep from running her down. She never spared him as much as a glance, for which Frank supposed he should be thankful, but wasn't. He'd have to have a talk with Bonanza Coombs about traffic safety....

Half a block up the other side of the street, Bonnie went into a small café. Habit had Frank note the name: Donna's Diner.

Maybe she worked there Thursday nights.

But Frank knew even before he'd parked the car and sauntered past its windows with his chin tucked into the stand-up collar of his jacket that she didn't. Not that he could see anything of what was happening inside or who was in there with the few furtive glances he tossed in as he passed.

He planted himself in the doorway of the building next door and waited for Bonnie to come out. He waited forty-two minutes and thirty-eight seconds. Seething with impatience, he verified the time just an instant before Bonnie emerged.

She turned toward the café's door to wait, then fell into step beside the tall, balding man with a briefcase who came out. They walked in the direction away from where Frank was pressing himself against the wall. He heard her laughing at something her companion said and felt a stab of pain as if someone had stuck a knife deep inside his back.

When had *he* ever made her laugh like that?

That day at the beach, that's when. She'd had fun with him there. Yeah, and later that day he'd made her cry.

He'd hurt her, but still.... What was she doing laughing and having fun with a middle-aged joker in an off-the-rack suit and tennis shoes?

He hung back, but kept the couple in sight. They walked side by side, obviously talking, though he was too far away to hear what was said. They never touched. A couple of blocks down the road, the guy stopped to let Bonnie precede him into a building.

Battling persistent suspicions, Frank looked around. The buildings in this block were mostly old-fashioned brick apartments. Something clutched at his gut, and he had to swallow down a surge of bitter bile. Apartments. The thought that flashed into his mind made his stomach turn.

Frank stopped walking and slapped a palm against the wall of the nearest building. A dog, skinny and unkempt, came sniffing around the corner. A couple of feet from where Frank stood, it lifted its leg and, a moment later, sauntered off.

Thinking the dog's behavior a fitting commentary, Frank turned and headed back to his car.

The street was one way, meaning he had to drive past the building into which Bonnie and her... friend had disappeared. Though he'd promised himself he wouldn't, Frank glanced at it. Red brick, much like the others. Old. Not in the best of shape. A group of women in sweats filed out of the wide open front door, laughing and screeching and beginning to run as the now pelting rain instantly drenched their clothes.

Thurston County Community Club.

Mother Murphy!

Swearing, Frank felt both weak with relief and shamed to his very soul as everything suddenly fell into

place. Bonnie taught art, didn't she? She taught at
Saint C's and was dedicated to her time there. No
doubt she taught here, too. The guy with the briefcase was either a student or one of the other instruc-
tors at this community club.

Why the hell couldn't she have just said so?

He pulled the car over and parked it along the curb.
So what if it said Absolutely No Parking? This
wouldn't take long.

Inside he asked a teenage boy with an armful of papers and books in which room the art class was being
taught.

The kid shrugged. "I dunno," he said sullenly, eyes
shifting here and there. "There's some people in that
room down the hall. Ask them." And then he took
off.

Frank watched the boy's departure with wry
thoughtfulness. Bet he's seen the inside of jail a time
or two before. Turning, he dismissed the kid from his
mind and walked down the hall to the room he'd indicated. The door was ajar. Frank peered through the
foot-wide opening.

Bonnie was sitting at a table next to the man from
the café. Their heads were close together. Bonnie was
reading aloud, and the man noddingly followed along.
Frank couldn't hear the words. Slowly, carefully, he
pushed at the door to widen the gap and duck
through.

The agonized and discordant squeak of a hinge in
need of oil sounded like a siren's screech in the still-
ness of the room. Frank froze with one foot across the
threshold, his body half in the room, half out.

Across the room, two heads lifted. Two startled pairs of eyes blinked at him. For interminable moments Bonnie's were locked on Frank's.

Feeling foolish, suddenly, he stepped all the way in. "Hi," he said with a grin that was a little uncertain in the face of the horror he saw gathering in Bonnie's expression. "Don't let me disturb— What the *hell...?* Bonanza!!"

But she'd already shouldered past him and was flying down the hall toward the exit as though demons pursued her. Shouting her name, Frank set out after her. But out on the street, she was nowhere to be seen.

"Hell and damn!" Frank swore, adding a string of choice words that turned the air blue and brought a look of admiration to the face of an old man walking by. Furious with himself and the way he had botched the entire venture, Frank ran back into the building.

The guy in the suit was at the door, glowering. "What's the meaning of this?" he demanded angrily as soon as Frank was within shouting distance. "Where's Bonanza?"

"Damned if I know." Frank was not in the mood to mince words. "Who're you? And what's going on here?"

The other man's scowl deepened. "Listen, sonny," he said with the kind of authority reserved for policemen, priests and schoolteachers. Frank wondered fleetingly to which of the three groups this man, now blistering his ears, belonged. "I'll ask the questions here. What's your name and who're you to Bonanza Coombs?"

Mutely, Frank pulled out his ID and, flipping the small leather folder open, showed his badge. "Frank Malloy," he said curtly. "Rivervale P.D."

The man took his time scrutinizing Frank's identification. Though incensed, Frank couldn't help but be impressed by his thoroughness. Here was a man not easily fooled. The sharp eyes with which he finally studied Frank reinforced that impression.

"Jack Trainer," the man finally introduced himself, adding, "Is, uh, Miss Coombs in some kind of trouble?"

"You tell me," Frank said.

"What...?" Trainer looked first confused, then taken aback. "You mean, in trouble *here?* Good God, man, all we're doing is *reading.* You saw that."

"Reading." Frank stared at the floor, puzzled. "So what's the big deal?" He directed the question more to himself than to Trainer.

But the other man answered anyhow. "The big deal," he said with quiet dignity and pride, "is that just a few months ago, Bonanza Coombs didn't know how to read. Now she does."

It was almost midnight by the time Frank heard the front door open and shut. He was out of Addie's kitchen and in the foyer, confronting Bonnie in one furious flash.

"Where the *hell* have you been?" Saints alive, the woman looked like a drowned cat. Not waiting for a reply, Frank grabbed her and hustled her into the bathroom.

"Strip!" he ordered, already bending over the tub and fiddling with the taps. Explanations could wait until after he'd gotten Bonnie into some hot water and dry clothes.

He straightened to find himself face-to-face with green-eyed indignation.

"Now you listen to me, Frank Malloy—" Though no longer in the outraged frame of mind she'd been in earlier, Bonnie decided she'd had just about enough of Frank's high-handedness for one day. "If you're not out of here in one second, I'm going to scream rape."

"So scream." Frank stepped around her, pulled down the zipper at the back of her dress and pulled the straps off her shoulders.

Bonnie crossed her arms to hold the sagging garment in place. Steam billowed from the tub, blinding the mirror and warming the air. Bonnie shivered.

"That does it," Frank announced, and in the same instant, he scooped Bonnie into his arms. Dress and all, he dumped her into the tub. "I'll see you when you're done."

"Don't bet on it!" Bonnie yelled after him, surging to her feet. "You big baboon!"

Frank had hot chocolate waiting when Bonnie finally came into the kitchen. He shot her a quick glance—she was wrapped in a ratty chenille robe with a towel, turban-style, covering her head—and he poured her a cup without speaking. He set it down in front of the captain's chair, into which she'd plopped.

"Thanks." Bonnie said the word grudgingly. She tucked up her feet and took a cautious sip. It warmed all the places the bath alone hadn't, though she conceded it might also be Frank's presence that was making her warm.

"Something to eat?" Frank asked.

Bonnie drew herself up, frowning as she looked around with exaggerated curiosity. "Is this *my* kitchen, or did I take a wrong turn somewhere?"

Frank ignored her. "How about I fix you some toast?"

Bonnie slumped. Sighing, she said, "No, thanks." She lowered her head. "Look, Frank, I know we have some things to talk about, but could it wait? I've had about all I can handle for one day."

"And I haven't?" He'd been going out of his mind for the past four hours, wondering if she was alive or dead. He gritted his teeth. "Just tell me this—why?"

"Oh, swell." Bonnie's head snapped up. "A simple question, right? Why *what*, Frank? Why couldn't I read? Why aren't I like other people? Why did I ever come here?" She looked away. "You think I haven't asked myself those questions a million times?"

"Well, I'm *not* asking them." Frank came to where Bonnie sat and gripped her upper arms. "I don't care about any of that. I care about *you.*"

For an instant, Bonnie's heart soared. It came back to earth with a thump when Frank added, "I care about your safety, and you should, too. It's a war zone out there, Bonanza. It's not safe to be out on the streets alone, never mind hitchhike—"

"I didn't hitchhike."

"Then how'd you get home? You left all your things behind when you ran like a yellow-bellied rabbit—"

Bonnie tried, unsuccessfully, to shake off Frank's hands. "Dammit, who gives you the right to call me names?"

"I do," Frank said brutally. "I calls 'em as I sees 'em, Bonanza. You're a coward."

"And you're a bully," Bonnie cried, shaking him off as she leapt to her feet. "Just like every other cop I've ever met." She shouldered past Frank and would have stomped out of the room had he not caught her arm.

"Oh, no, you don't." He spun her around to face him. "You're not going to run this time, Bonnie."

She stiffened, her mouth opened to let fly another heated rejoinder. But something in Frank's eyes— some residue of pain; he'd worried about her—made her shut it again. She closed her eyes and shudderingly exhaled the breath she'd taken for her unvoiced tirade.

"I'm sorry I worried you," she said finally, opening her eyelids and looking into his eyes, wanting nothing so much as to melt into his arms and say, Love me, Frank. I love you so. "Lloyd Soames was driving the eleven o'clock bus. He knows me by now. He let me ride for free."

Frank nodded, but didn't let her go. "I would've understood, Bonnie," he said. "Why didn't you tell me you couldn't read?"

"I didn't tell anybody. I ask you—" Bonnie pulled a wry face. "Would *you* have broadcasted a thing like that?"

Frank let go of her arm. He wanted to hug her, feel her against him, safe and sound. He made no move to do so. It was Bonnie's turn—probably long overdue—to call the shots. "Telling someone you're close to isn't the same as broadcasting, Bonanza."

She went to stand by the stove. Picking up the wooden spoon, she absently stirred the skin off the cooling chocolate milk. "Are we close, Frank?" she asked in a small voice.

"I want us to be."

"Why?"

"Because I love you."

"Oh, Frank." The spoon fell into the pot with a *thunk*. Bonnie gripped the edge of the range as her chin dropped onto her chest.

Frank was behind her now. He encircled her waist, pulled her against his body. "Marry me, Bonnie," he whispered, nuzzling the back of her neck.

"I want to." Frank could hardly make out the words, Bonnie spoke them so softly, but his heart soared at the sound of them. "I love you so much."

Slowly, she turned to look at him with brimming eyes. "I love you, Frank—"

They kissed. Tenderly, lips brushing lips. Deeply, tongues touching, stroking, entwining. Lightly, withdrawing, teasing with little nips and bites.

"I'll always love you," Bonnie whispered. "But I do know now that . . . I can't marry you."

Chapter Eleven

For a moment Frank thought Bonnie was joking. He started to laugh. But when she didn't join in, when, instead, tears gathered at the corners of her eyes and her chin wobbled, he sobered. "You're serious."

Bonnie bit down hard on her bottom lip and glanced down at the floor. Mutely, she nodded.

Frank frowned. "You said you loved me."

Bonnie swallowed bitter tears. "I do."

"So then—" Breaking off, Frank gave his head a brisk shake, as if to clear it. "I don't understand."

"God." With a half sob, half laugh, Bonnie turned away. She looked up at the ceiling. "I'm not surprised." She swallowed again. Tears were pooling at the back of her throat this time. "I don't understand it myself. But still . . ."

She drew a shuddering breath and slowly faced him. "I know I'm right to say this, Frank. Getting married is for life. Or at least, I'd want it to be. . . ."

"You think I don't? Is that it?" Frank interrupted. "Are you afraid we'll break up a few years down the line?"

"No." She meant it; he'd be steady. "No, not really."

"Then what?"

Bonnie sighed. "I took a good look at myself tonight when I was wandering around. And I got to thinking that every time I've messed up, it's been when I've been on my own. I only did good when I had people to lean on. First there was Ellie." She looked down at her hands, at the fingers she was twisting into knots, and then back up at Frank. "Here, I've leaned on you. I've come to need you—"

"What's wrong with that?" Frank asked urgently. "I've come to need you, too."

"But not the same way," Bonnie cried, "don't you see? It scares me to death, the idea of being on my own, of having nobody to love and nobody who loves me. It scares me so much that I'd do almost anything, say almost anything rather than be alone again. I've been so lonely. . . ."

She buried her face in her hands.

Frank looked down at the top of her head with a mixture of dismay, confusion and anger. "Are you telling me," he said slowly, wrestling with the incongruity of it all as he talked, "that you...that you said you loved me only because you're afraid of being alone, and you figured saying the words will tie me to you?"

"No!" Her head jerked up. "No, Frank." But as they looked at each other in the silence that followed, her expression of dismayed denial turned into a troubled frown. "Yes," she said, her eyes on his. "Maybe." Slowly, she lowered her hands, and her shoulders dropped. "I don't know."

She turned away, picked up a mug of now cold chocolate, sniffed it, set it down. Behind her she could hear Frank scrape aside a chair as he walked to the window. She was hurting him, she knew. But she couldn't help it.

"That's what I've got to find out, Frank," she said without turning. "Don't you see?"

"I see." Looking out into the rainy darkness, what he saw was that without Bonnie in his future, the days ahead loomed as bleak and dreary as this night. If he'd ever felt this terrible before, he couldn't recall when. He'd never told a woman he loved her; he'd never been rejected, either. He didn't like losing, and it wasn't his way to give up without a fight.

He cleared his throat. "So, ah..." The frog was still there. Turning, he cleared his throat again. "So what if I told you," he said to Bonnie's back, "that I don't care about what you said. What if I was willing to take the chance it'll all work out and wanted to marry you anyway?"

He'd never begged before; he didn't like it. But he had to know. "Would you?"

Slowly, Bonnie turned around, too. Looking at Frank, the expression she saw on his face—a desolate sort of entreaty warring with something darker—made her bite down hard on her lower lip. Still, she shook her head.

"Why not?" Frank's tone was harsh with frustration. Dammit, she loved him; she'd said so. He'd felt it. Hell, he could feel it even now as she stood there stubbornly shaking her head. "A chance, that's all I'm asking. Why won't you at least give it that?"

"Because it's wrong," she cried. "Because you deserve better, and I do, too. I want to *be* somebody, Frank. I need to make something of myself before I become just some man's missus. I want—"

Frank tuned her out. *Just some man's missus.* If she'd taken a gun and shot a bullet through his heart, she couldn't have hurt him more. Without another word, he walked out of Addie Filmore's kitchen.

The next morning, carrying an armload of clothes, he walked out of Bonanza Coombs's life.

Some guys with a truck came later that day to get his furniture. Just before dark, Marie Donelly came with Frank's key and a check for four months' rent.

Bonnie tore up the check on the spot. She didn't want Frank to pay. If he hadn't left of his own accord—though she'd hoped under happier circumstances—she would have asked him to move out. She wanted the house to herself. She wanted to take care of it herself and rely on no one but herself. She'd resolved not to touch another dime of her grandmother's legacy.

Jack Trainer had pronounced her a competent reader. Fine. From here on in all she needed was practice to polish her skills, and next week she was scheduled to take a GED test. If she passed—and Jack, with whom she'd been preparing for it, had no doubt she would—she was getting herself a job. She had it all planned out.

What she hadn't planned on was the heartache. It had started with the *whoosh* of the kitchen door closing, and it wasn't just an ache in the heart. It was an all-pervading pain, a burning and twisting in all of Bonnie's vital organs, that stole her appetite and robbed her of sleep.

She told herself it would only hurt for a little while.

"You look pale," Marie remarked, seating herself at the kitchen table without an invitation. "About the same shade of green, in fact, that my brother was sporting when he brought me the key."

"Don't raz me today, Marie. Please." Bonnie wiped the already spotless counter yet again. She'd gotten up at dawn and scrubbed the entire kitchen.

"Just stating the facts, ma'am. You got any coffee?"

"I'm really very busy, Marie." Bonnie rinsed the rag.

"Why don't I make us some?" Marie was already on her feet and, squeezing in next to Bonnie at the sink, filling the coffeemaker with water. "I'm sure we could both use a cup."

Bonnie faced her. "I don't want to talk, if that's what this is leading to."

Marie's eyebrows rose. She spooned coffee into the filter and turned on the machine. "At all?"

"Well..." Lately Marie had more and more become a friend and confidante. A sort of substitute for Ellie, which was precisely the kind of dependency Bonnie wanted to get away from. She knew that Marie was itching to find out and discuss whatever had gone

wrong between Bonnie and Frank. "Not about anything . . . important."

"How about the weather?"

Bonnie's smile was wan. She tossed down the rag
and sat down. "Sounds good."

"Nice day, isn't it?"

"No."

"No?" Marie, setting mugs on the table, shot Bonnie a sideways glance. "Last time I looked, the sun
was shining."

"Do you think I could get a job here in town?"
Bonnie asked, voicing one of her worries. She told
herself she only wanted Marie's opinion. She wasn't
leaning on her in any way.

Marie pursed her lips but made no comment about
the shift in conversational direction. She sat down
across from Bonnie. "I guess that depends on what
your skills are."

Bonnie grimaced. "Zip, pretty much."

"There's your art."

"My work's not good enough to sell." The coffee
was done. Bonnie got up to pour it. "Not yet, anyway."

"You might try for a job at Swain's Hobby Shop."

"Hmm." Bonnie pushed cream and sugar toward
Marie. "I want to go to college, Marie. I'm taking the
GED test."

"I bet you'll do great. What do you want to study
in college?"

"Early-childhood education."

"You're a natural for that, Bon."

"I can do the first two years of it at the community
college right here in town, Jack Trainer told me."

"Who's Jack Trainer?"

Bonnie told her, ending with a hesitant, "Frank, uh, met him last night."

Marie set her mug down so hard, some coffee swamped over onto the table. She leaned toward Bonnie with a frown. "Don't tell me this mess has to do with your reading?"

"No." Bonnie got up, went to stand by the window. In the Savages' yard, Jimmy was trimming the hedge. "He asked me to marry him."

Again Marie didn't comment on Bonnie's conversational shift. She sighed. "Why do I get the feeling this isn't a happy tale?"

"I told him I couldn't."

"I see." Another sigh. "You don't love him."

Bonnie said nothing. She looked down at her hands. "How old were you when you got married, Marie?"

With a short, wry laugh Marie said, "I was a baby, just out of high school. Michael was a junior in college." She shook her head and laughed again. "God, we were dumb. So dumb we even ended up working together. Mike was a cop, too, you see."

Bonnie turned. "Would you do it again?"

"Oh, yeah." Marie, sad now, nodded. "I'd do it all again in a minute." She looked at Bonnie and twisted her lips into not quite a smile. "Since none of us know how long we've got on this earth, I figure we owe it to ourselves to grab all the happiness we can."

While Bonnie didn't exactly ace the GED test, she passed it sufficiently well to receive her certificate. With it in hand, she went to see an admissions coun-

selor at the college and, with surprisingly little cere-
mony, found herself enrolled.

It was the proudest moment of her life.

Feeling ten feet tall and on a roll, she stopped next
at Swain's Hobby Shop and asked for a part-time job.
They were sorry, but . . .

So were the owners of the stationery store, the video
rentals and the Fit-U-Boutique. Bonnie didn't even try
the drugstore.

The day was rapidly losing its shine. Her feet ached.
She crossed the street to Denman's Café.

Waitress Wanted.

"You're hired."

Could there be sweeter words in the dictionary?
Bonnie wondered, hurrying home. She was to start
work that night. Five to eight-thirty, the dinner shift.

In the foyer, at the foot of the stairs up to Frank's
empty apartment, the answer struck her—three words
spoken by the man you loved: *I love you.* Those words
were sweeter still.

She sat down on the stairs and cried.

Bonnie had only broken three plates in the week
she'd been working at Denman's, and she'd only
mixed up orders twice. The customers liked her, and
so did her boss. School would start in another two
weeks. She still volunteered at Saint C's and tutored
Jennifer twice a week. Her life was chock-full.

So how come it felt so empty?

She'd accomplished so much in the last little while,
and all on her own. She ought to be so proud, so
happy.

So how come she was so sad all the time?

She'd bought herself a bicycle to get around on, paying for it with her first paycheck. She'd joined the public library, read everything she could get her hands on, including Michener—she could take him or leave him—and even the manual that had come with the cable she'd had installed.

She had her life in shape; she was in charge. She knew where she was going.

So how come she felt so lost all the time? And why did the heartache which was really a body ache not get any better? Why did missing Frank just keep getting worse?

Frank told himself that the only reason he drove by Denman's Café every night was because that was the fastest way home. Maybe not the shortest, but the fastest. There were only three lights along Main, while Ashwood had four.

Driving by, he saw Bonnie twice. And each time it had taken a conscious act of will not to stop the car, run to her and shake her so hard, her teeth rattled. A more pigheaded and contrary female, Frank could swear, he'd never met.

Between Marie, Jennifer—he wasn't above milking his niece for information—his mom and Father Joe, Frank was kept up-to-date on what Bonnie was up to. He had to hand it to her, the woman had moxie. She also had smarts, talent—and a grip on his heart that he couldn't shake off.

Not that he hadn't tried. After all, there were plenty of women out there who'd kill to be "some man's missus." For instance, both Vera Tipkes and Delores Swanson had been delighted to be asked out by him.

He'd taken Vera to dinner and Delores to the theater all the way in Seattle.

Vera had asked him back up to her place for coffee and..."whatever." Her word. Frank had declined.

Delores had suggested they not make the almost two-hour drive back to Rivervale after the show and, instead, take a room in town somewhere. He'd declined that offer, too.

Truth to tell, the only "whatever" or room sharing he cared to do was with Bonanza Coombs.

He hadn't seen her tonight on his way home. In a foul mood, depressed before he'd even opened the door to the bright and generously proportioned modern apartment that was now his home, and which both he and Sam detested, Frank swore beneath his breath. How had he gotten to this pass? What was he doing here, alone and lonely, when just a couple of miles away lived the woman with whom he wanted to spend his life?

How could he convince her he needed to go back there? To the house. And to her.

He crossed the living room, tugging off his tie and flinging it over the back of the sofa. His jacket followed. He was rolling up his shirtsleeves, moodily wondering if he should fix himself a Scotch, maybe drink himself into a nice stupor, when Sam shot out from under the sofa and neatly tripped him up.

Swearing roundly, Frank regained his balance just short of falling on his face. "So help me, cat . . ."

Cat.

An idea blossomed and on Frank's face, a smile. "Sam, old buddy, get over here. . . ."

* * *

The doorbell rang. Bonnie, just out of her bath and on her way to bed, frowned at the clock. Who on earth would come calling at eleven-thirty at night?

Glancing down at the T-shirt that covered her loosely to the knees, she decided she was decent enough to open the door.

"Frank." She could no more stop the delight at seeing him from showing on her face than she could stop her heart from running amok in her chest. "And—" Bonnie frowned, cluing in now to Frank's somber expression "—Sam."

Only the cat's face was peeking out from the blanket in which he was wrapped. Bonnie's heart constricted.

"Oh, Frank. Is—is he sick?"

Frank bit his lip, slowly nodded. "Broken heart, the doctors say. He's pining."

Bonnie knew all about pining. She'd done a lot of it herself lately. "Oh, Frank. I feel so bad for him."

"Don't," Frank said. "You did what you thought was right." He stretched his neck, looked around the foyer. "You alone?"

"Of course."

Relief made Frank almost drop the cat. It'd been all he could do to restrain Sam as it was. "Could we come in?"

"I was just on my way to bed." But she stepped back and opened the door.

Frank took that as another positive sign. Her mile-wide smile at seeing him had been the first. He came inside. "That's my shirt you're wearing."

He loved the way Bonnie blushed. "I, umm…" She shrugged awkwardly. "I found it upstairs. I, uh—well, I thought you probably didn't want it…."

"But you did?"

Bonnie was sort of ambling toward the kitchen, and Frank followed.

Her flush became pronounced, and she averted her eyes. "Well…" She was walking half sideways, half backward. Now she banged into the wall and balefully glared at it as if it had moved into her path. "Well, it's comfortable."

"Comfortable" was not what Frank wanted anything regarding him to be for Bonnie. Exciting, yes. Irritating, fine. Welcome—now there was a word.

"You're welcome to keep it."

They were at the kitchen door now. The exchange with Bonnie had loosened Frank's grip on the cat. Sam wriggled once, twice—and was a flash of orange and white on his way out the nearest open window.

"Oh, look," Bonnie whispered, touched to the heart. "He's his old self again."

Frank said nothing. When Bonnie raised questioning eyes, he said, "Being here with you, so am I."

Tears—Lord, but Bonnie was tired of them. Still, there they were, shooting up into her eyes. "Oh, Frank…"

He touched her cheek. Caught a drop of moisture there. "I've missed you something awful, Bon."

She closed her eyes. She'd dreamed of this moment. Time and again she'd envisioned Frank coming here, saying things like, "I've missed you. I can't live without you. Marry me, Bonnie. Please, *please*, marry me…."

And this time she'd say, "Yes, my darling. I'm ready for you now. I've made my way. I've proved to myself I can do it." And then they'd live happily ever after. Just like in the movies.

Except this wasn't the movies. And what Bonanza said was, "Oh, Frank, I've been so miserable."

Without a word, Frank kissed her, pouring into the kiss all his emotions, everything he felt. It was a healing kiss, a kiss they both sorely needed. They touched not in passion, but in ways that reassured each of them the other was really there. For long moments they gave themselves up to the joy of it, and then they drew apart.

Bonnie had been the first to withdraw. Now she pulled out a chair, but instead of sitting, stood staring down at her hands on the back of it.

"Frank..." she began tentatively.

"Hmm?" Clearing his throat, feeling suddenly as awkward as Bonnie looked, Frank helped himself to a glass of water.

"Now what?" Bonnie asked. "Where do we go from here?"

"Straight to the altar, far as I'm concerned. Unless you're still not ready to become just 'some man's missus.'"

"Oh, Frank." Bonnie flew to his side and hugged him. "I didn't mean for that to hurt you. It came out all wrong. I only meant—"

"Shh." Frank laid a finger over her lips, then put his mouth there in a quick kiss. "I think I know what you meant. You needed some space...."

"Yes."

"You needed to find yourself."

"Yes. I know that sounds clichéd, but—"

"No, it doesn't." Frank smoothed a silky strand of hair off her face, then let his hand linger in a gentle caress. "And once I got over my injured pride, I understood."

He kissed her nose. "You've made yourself into one helluva lady, Bonanza Coombs, but something tells me this is only the beginning."

"Oh, Frank." Framing his face with her hands, Bonnie looked deeply into his eyes. "I could never have done it on my own—"

"Yes, you could. You did."

"But I came to understand it doesn't matter, you see?"

Barely listening as Bonnie went on to explain how she'd learned that no person was an island, what Frank saw was a confident, glowing young woman who any man would be proud to call his partner. But she was his. His heart sang.

Suddenly desperate for her, he stopped her speech with a hard, fiery kiss. "How you do go on," he whispered against her lips, before losing himself in another long kiss. "When'll you get to the good part?"

Bonnie's head was spinning. "The good part?"

"The part where you say, 'I love you, Frank.'"

"Oh." Bonnie's lips curved seductively. Her tongue delved into the cleft of his chin. "That part." She teased the corners of his mouth. "I wrote it in a letter. Want me to get it for you?"

"No." Frank's arms tightened around her.

"It's in my bedroom...."

"Oh...?" The gleam in his eyes turned to fire. "Well, in that case." He swung her up into his arms and walked toward the door.

Her heart pounding, every nerve alive and tingling, Bonnie wound her arms around Frank's neck and hung on. She nuzzled his cheek, bit his ear. And then she whispered, "I love you, Frank."

They were in the hall. Frank stopped walking. His mouth found hers, and time stood still.

* * * * *

Silhouette
R O M A N C E™

HEARTLAND HOLIDAYS

Christmas bells turn into wedding bells for the Gallagher siblings in Stella Bagwell's *Heartland Holidays* trilogy.

THEIR FIRST THANKSGIVING (#903) in November
Olivia Westcott had once rejected Sam Gallagher's proposal—and in his stubborn pride, he'd refused to hear her reasons why. Now Olivia is back...and it is about time Sam Gallagher listened!

THE BEST CHRISTMAS EVER (#909) in December
Soldier Nick Gallagher had come home to be the best man at his brother's wedding—not to be a groom! But when he met single mother Allison Lee, he knew he'd found his bride.

NEW YEAR'S BABY (#915) in January
Kathleen Gallagher had given up on love and marriage until she came to the rescue of neighbor Ross Douglas . . . and the newborn baby he'd found on his doorstep!

Come celebrate the holidays with Silhouette Romance!

Silhouette Christmas Stories 1992

Experience the beauty of Yuletide romance with Silhouette Christmas Stories 1992—a collection of heartwarming stories by favorite Silhouette authors.

> JONI'S MAGIC by Mary Lynn Baxter
> HEARTS OF HOPE by Sondra Stanford
> THE NIGHT SANTA CLAUS RETURNED by Marie Ferrarrella
> BASKET OF LOVE by Jeanne Stephens

Also available this year are three popular early editions of Silhouette Christmas Stories—1986, 1987 and 1988. Look for these and you'll be well on your way to a complete collection of the best in holiday romance.

Plus, as an added bonus, you can receive a FREE keepsake Christmas ornament. Just collect four proofs of purchase from any November or December 1992 Harlequin or Silhouette series novels, or from any Harlequin or Silhouette Christmas collection, and receive a beautiful dated brass Christmas candle ornament.

Mail this certificate along with four (4) proof-of-purchase coupons, plus $1.50 postage and handling (check or money order—do not send cash), payable to Silhouette Books, to: **In the U.S.:** P.O. Box 9057, Buffalo, NY 14269-9057; **In Canada:** P.O. Box 622, Fort Erie, Ontario, L2A 5X3.

ONE PROOF OF PURCHASE

SX92POP

Name: _____

_____

Address: _____

_____

City: _____

State/Province: _____

Zip/Postal Code: _____

093 KAG